The Tragedy of Hamlet, Prince of Denmark

The Annotated Edition

THE

Tragicall Hiſtorie of

HAMLET,

Prince of Denmarke.

By William Shakeſpeare.

Newly imprinted and enlarged to almoſt as much
againe as it was, according to the true and perfect
Coppie.

AT LONDON,
Printed by I. R. for N. L. and are to be ſold at his
ſhoppe vnder Saint Dunſtons Church in
Fleetſtreet. 1605.

INTRODUCTION

Hamlet is not only William Shakespeare's most well known play, it is the most well known and performed play in the entire English language. Early drafts of the play date back to 1603, making it a nearly 400 year old spectacle that continues to delight, confound, capture, and engage (or enrage?) casual readers and students alike. At its basic form, *Hamlet* tells the story of a young man struggling in the throes of a mental breakdown while on the path toward revenge. This tale of heavy emotion and turmoil has captured the hearts and minds of audiences for centuries. What is it about this particular play that has left such a mark? Read more to find out.

With this version of the text, our intention is make Shakespeare's beloved play not only accessible to casual readers, but also enjoyable. It is our hope that reading through the full authentic text (with a multitude of guiding notes) will inspire you to continue your study of *Hamlet* and your exploration of Shakespeare in general. As such, we have included in our supplementary annotations several notes concerning interpretations, themes, symbols, and deeper meanings of the text.

This *Annotated Edition* of Hamlet is a simple reproduction of the generally accepted text with words and phrases glossed for easy understanding and simple comprehension by even the most casual of readers. Each of the play's five acts are accompanied by both a summary and an assessment to help guide readers through the events of the play. A final discussion guide is included at the end of the text (which may also serve as a list of potential paper topics for students still in school).

A NOTE ON READING AND UNDERSTANDING SHAKESPEAREAN LANGUAGE

We're not going to lie, reading the language of William Shakespeare can be difficult at times, even to the most educated scholars. But don't despair! Feeling slightly puzzled is part of the process. Anyone who claims to have a clear and full understanding of every single line right from the first read is trying to impress you. Most of us need a little help along the way.

Remember, much of what you will read of Shakespeare was originally written to be performed, meaning that actors would be the ones to illuminate many of the vagaries and nuances within the text. Additionally, these words are nearly 400 years old, and are full of slang and common phrases well known to their original audiences. Think about how much common language has changed just over the past year. We should be thankful that there's anything left of Shakespeare's that we can call English in the first place! But we do promise that the text is English. Read and digest it slowly. Use the summaries and notes as guide rails.

The language of Shakespeare can be tough to grasp because it is old, yes, but also because, well, William Shakespeare was a *really really* good writer. He loved playing word games and writing riddles. He excelled at crafting twists and turns of linguistic combinations. He was a poet after all, and part of the job of the poet is to challenge the conventions of language. How much meaning can words hold? What is the best way to shape linguistic form to emotion? Shakespeare loved using his plays and works as a means to explore these questions as well.

As a result, you'll notice moments in the play where Shakespeare may have felt creatively moved to the extent of favoring poetic or linguistic flair over straightforward, easy to read content. So the interpretive task of the modern student becomes two fold—first decode the language itself, then decode the flair.

We have done our best to distinguish between language and flair in our explanatory notes, but do not feel too put out if you simply find yourself lost at times. To be overwhelmed by a cascade of language, sound, device, and meaning is simply part of the experience, and part of why reading and rereading becomes a joy over the years.

Not only will your understanding of the text grow as you develop a better handle on the content, but your enjoyment will continue to grow as you develop a deeper awareness of yourself as a reader, scholar, and even as a person.

SETTING THE SCENE FOR HAMLET

Hamlet enters our tale as a young man described, in the play's subtitle, as the "Prince of Denmark." His father, King Hamlet, has just recently died and much to young Hamlet's dismay, his mother (Queen Gertrude) has chosen to marry Hamlet's uncle (Claudius). To make matters worse, Claudius has also decided to claim the crown of Denmark for himself, and now rules as king. Hamlet is very distressed by all of this and struggles deeply, until he is visited by a shadowy figure who appears to be the ghost of his father…

The Tragedy of Hamlet, Prince of Denmark

DRAMATIS PERSONAE

HAMLET, son of the former King Hamlet

KING CLAUDIUS, King of Denmark

QUEEN GERTRUDE, Queen of Denmark

HORATIO, Hamlet's friend and classmate

POLONIUS, councilman of King Claudius

OPHELIA, daughter of Polonius

LAERTES, son of Polonius

REYNOLDO, a servant

GHOST, ghost of King Hamlet, Hamlet's father

ROSENCRANTZ, & GUILDENSTERN, other classmates

FRANCISCO, MARCELLUS & BERNARDO, sentry men

FORTINBRAS, Prince of Norway

CAPTAIN, of Norway

VOLTEMAND & CORNELIUS, ambassadors to Norway

OSRIC, a courtier

PLAYERS, theater performers

GRAVEDIGGER, a clown

SECOND MAN, another clown

ACT I SUMMARY

Act I does what is common in many of Shakespeare's plays—it introduces the setting, characters, and the motions of a plot at work. We enter our story on a cold night on the guard platform of Lake Elsinore castle, the home of the King and Queen of Denmark, and also Hamlet. Hamlet has been away at school in Wittenberg, but has recently returned home. A pair of watchmen spot a strange figure shimmering in the distance, but they don't know what it could be. They try to speak to it, but it gives no reply.

From there, we meet our main character Hamlet during a gathering with his family. They chide him for being so moody in the wake of his father's death and this only makes him moodier. It's almost as if the world continues on without him, unaware of his grief and pain. However, his best friend Horatio comes to find him and tells him about the strange figure seen along the guard platform.

We also meet up with Polonius, a courtier, and his two children, Laertes and Ophelia. Ophelia confides in her brother about Hamlet's affections toward her. But Laertes soon warns her not to take him too seriously. Polonius echoes the warning with strong words of his own.

The act ends where we began, with the re-emergence of the strange figure that began the story. It beckons Hamlet to follow, and he chases after it.

ACT I: Scene I

SCENE I. Elsinore. A platform before the castle.

[FRANCISCO at his post. Enter to him BERNARDO]

BERNARDO: Who's there?

FRANCISCO: Nay, answer me: stand, and unfold yourself.

BERNARDO: Long live the king!

FRANCISCO: Bernardo?

BERNARDO: He.

FRANCISCO: You come most carefully upon your hour.

BERNARDO: 'Tis now struck twelve; get thee to bed, Francisco.

FRANCISCO: For this relief much thanks: 'tis bitter cold,

And I am sick at heart.

BERNARDO: Have you had quiet guard?

FRANCISCO: Not a mouse stirring.

BERNARDO: Well, good night.

If you do meet Horatio and Marcellus,

The rivals of my watch, bid them make haste.

FRANCISCO: I think I hear them. Stand, ho! Who's there?

[Enter HORATIO and MARCELLUS]

HORATIO: Friends to this ground.

MARCELLUS: And liegemen to the Dane.

FRANCISCO: Give you good night.

MARCELLUS: O, farewell, honest soldier:

Who hath relieved you?

FRANCISCO: Bernardo has my place.

Give you good night.

[Exit]

MARCELLUS: Holla! Bernardo!

BERNARDO: Say,

What, is Horatio there?

HORATIO: A piece of him.

BERNARDO: Welcome, Horatio: welcome, good Marcellus.

MARCELLUS: What, has this thing appear'd again to-night?

BERNARDO: I have seen nothing.

MARCELLUS: Horatio says 'tis but our fantasy,

And will not let belief take hold of him

Touching this dreaded sight, twice seen of us:

Therefore I have entreated him along

With us to watch the minutes of this night;

That if again this apparition come,

He may approve our eyes and speak to it.

HORATIO: Tush, tush, 'twill not appear.

BERNARDO: Sit down awhile;

And let us once again assail your ears,

That are so fortified against our story[1]

What we have two nights seen.

HORATIO: Well, sit we down,

And let us hear Bernardo speak of this.

BERNARDO: Last night of all,

When yond same star that's westward from the pole

Had made his course to illume that part of heaven

---

[1] We will tell you once again this tale that you are so determined not to believe

Where now it burns, Marcellus and myself,

The bell then beating one—

[Enter Ghost]

MARCELLUS: Peace, break thee off; look, where it comes again!

BERNARDO: In the same figure, like the king that's dead.

MARCELLUS: Thou art a scholar; speak to it, Horatio[2].

BERNARDO: Looks it not like the king? mark it, Horatio.

HORATIO: Most like: it harrows[3] me with fear and wonder.

BERNARDO: It would[4] be spoke to.

MARCELLUS: Question it, Horatio.

HORATIO: What art thou that usurp'st this time of night,

Together with that fair and warlike form

In which the majesty of buried Denmark

Did sometimes march? by heaven I charge thee, speak!

MARCELLUS: It is offended.

BERNARDO: See, it stalks away!

HORATIO: Stay! speak, speak! I charge thee, speak!

[Exit Ghost]

MARCELLUS: 'Tis gone, and will not answer.

BERNARDO: How now, Horatio! you tremble and look pale:

Is not this something more than fantasy?

What think you on't?

HORATIO: Before my God, I might not this believe

Without the sensible and true avouch

---

[2] It was believed that educated individuals could commune with ghosts (Hudson)

[3] Fills

[4] Should

Of mine own eyes.

MARCELLUS: Is it not like the king?

HORATIO: As thou art to thyself:

Such was the very armour he had on

When he the ambitious Norway combated;

So frown'd he once, when, in an angry parle,

He smote the sledded Polacks on the ice.

'Tis strange.

MARCELLUS: Thus twice before, and jump[5] at this dead hour,

With martial stalk hath he gone by our watch.

HORATIO: In what particular thought to work I know not;

But in the gross and scope of my opinion,

This bodes some strange eruption to our state.

MARCELLUS: Good now, sit down, and tell me, he that knows,

Why this same strict and most observant watch

So nightly toils the subject of the land,

And why such daily cast of brazen cannon,

And foreign mart for implements of war;

Why such impress of shipwrights, whose sore task

Does not divide the Sunday from the week;

What might be toward, that this sweaty haste

Doth make the night joint-labourer with the day:

Who is't that can inform me?

HORATIO: That can I;

At least, the whisper goes so. Our last king,

Whose image even but now appear'd to us,

Was, as you know, by Fortinbras of Norway,

---

[5] *jump* is used for *just* (Hudson)

Thereto prick'd on by a most emulate pride,

Dared to the combat; in which our valiant Hamlet—

For so this side of our known world esteem'd him—

Did slay this Fortinbras; who by a seal'd compact,

Well ratified by law and heraldry,

Did forfeit, with his life, all those his lands

Which he stood seized of, to the conqueror:

Against the which, a moiety[6] competent

Was gaged by our king; which had return'd

To the inheritance of Fortinbras,

Had he been vanquisher; as, by the same covenant,

And carriage of the article design'd,

His fell to Hamlet. Now, sir, young Fortinbras,

Of unimproved mettle[7] hot and full,

Hath in the skirts of Norway here and there

Shark'd[8] up a list of lawless resolutes,

For food and diet, to some enterprise

That hath a stomach[9] in't; which is no other—

As it doth well appear unto our state—

But to recover of us, by strong hand

And terms compulsatory, those foresaid lands

So by his father lost: and this, I take it,

Is the main motive of our preparations,

The source of this our watch and the chief head

---

[6] equivalent portion (Hudson)

[7] *Unimproved mettle* to mean *untested spirit* (see Hudson)

[8] *"Drew up"* a list

[9] Courage

Of this post-haste and romage in the land[10].

BERNARDO: I think it be no other but e'en so:

Well may it sort that this portentous figure

Comes armed through our watch; so like the king

That was and is the question of these wars.

HORATIO: A mote it is to trouble the mind's eye.

In the most high and palmy[11] state of Rome,

A little ere the mightiest Julius fell,

The graves stood tenantless and the sheeted dead

Did squeak and gibber in the Roman streets:

As stars with trains of fire and dews of blood,

Disasters in the sun; and the moist star

Upon whose influence Neptune's empire stands

Was sick almost to doomsday with eclipse:

And even the like precurse of fierce events,

As harbingers preceding still the fates

And prologue to the omen coming on,

Have heaven and earth together demonstrated

Unto our climatures and countrymen.—

But soft, behold! lo, where it comes again!

[Re-enter Ghost]

I'll cross it, though it blast me. Stay, illusion!

If thou hast any sound, or use of voice,

Speak to me:

If there be any good thing to be done,

---

[10] This is a vague and hasty rundown of a political subplot that will run beneath much of the story. Denmark has a rival in the Norwegian prince called Fortinbras and it is known that he is making slow advance toward the kingdom

[11] Victorious

That may to thee do ease and grace to me,

Speak to me:

If thou art privy to thy country's fate,

Which, happily, foreknowing may avoid, O, speak!

Or if thou hast uphoarded in thy life

Extorted treasure in the womb of earth,

For which, they say, you spirits oft walk in death,

Speak of it: stay, and speak! Stop it, Marcellus.

[Cock crows]

MARCELLUS: Shall I strike at it with my partisan[12]?

HORATIO: Do, if it will not stand.

BERNARDO: 'Tis here!

HORATIO: 'Tis here!

MARCELLUS: 'Tis gone!

[Exit Ghost]

We do it wrong, being so majestical,

To offer it the show of violence;

For it is, as the air, invulnerable,

And our vain blows malicious mockery.

BERNARDO: It was about to speak, when the cock crew.

HORATIO: And then it started like a guilty thing

Upon a fearful summons. I have heard,

The cock, that is the trumpet to the morn,

Doth with his lofty and shrill-sounding throat

Awake the god of day; and, at his warning,

Whether in sea or fire, in earth or air,

The extravagant and erring spirit hies

---

[12] **Spear**

To his confine: and of the truth herein

This present object made probation[13].

MARCELLUS: It faded on the crowing of the cock.

Some say that ever 'gainst that season comes

Wherein our Saviour's birth is celebrated,

The bird of dawning singeth all night long:

And then, they say, no spirit dares stir abroad;

The nights are wholesome; then no planets strike,

No fairy takes, nor witch hath power to charm,

So hallow'd and so gracious is the time.

HORATIO: So have I heard and do in part believe it.

But, look, the morn, in russet mantle clad,

Walks o'er the dew of yon high eastward hill:

Break we our watch up; and by my advice,

Let us impart what we have seen to-night

Unto young Hamlet; for, upon my life,

This spirit, dumb to us, will speak to him.

Do you consent we shall acquaint him with it,

As needful in our loves, fitting our duty?

MARCELLUS: Let's do't, I pray; and I this morning know

Where we shall find him most conveniently.

[Exeunt]

---

[13] Proof

ACT I: SCENE II

SCENE II. Elsinore Castle

[Enter KING CLAUDIUS, QUEEN GERTRUDE, HAMLET, POLONIUS, LAERTES, VOLTEMAND, CORNELIUS, Lords, and Attendants]

KING CLAUDIUS: Though yet of Hamlet our dear brother's death

The memory be green, and that it us befitted

To bear our hearts in grief and our whole kingdom

To be contracted in one brow of woe,

Yet so far hath discretion fought with nature

That we with wisest sorrow think on him,

Together with remembrance of ourselves.

Therefore our sometime[1] sister, now our queen,

The imperial jointress[2] to this warlike state,

Have we, as 'twere with a defeated joy,

With an auspicious and a dropping eye,

With mirth in funeral and with dirge in marriage,

In equal scale weighing delight and dole,

Taken to wife: nor have we herein barr'd

Your better wisdoms, which have freely gone

With this affair along. For all, our thanks.

Now follows, that you know, young Fortinbras,

Holding a weak supposal of our worth,

Or thinking by our late dear brother's death

---

[1] At one time; "This woman who was at one time our sister and is now..." (see Hudson)

[2] Heiress

Our state to be disjoint[3] and out of frame,

Colleagued with the dream of his advantage,

He hath not fail'd to pester us with message,

Importing the surrender of those lands

Lost by his father, with all bonds[4] of law,

To our most valiant brother. So much for him.

Now for ourself and for this time of meeting:

Thus much the business is: we have here writ

To Norway, uncle of young Fortinbras,

Who, impotent and bed-rid, scarcely hears

Of this his nephew's purpose,—to suppress

His further gait herein; in that the levies,

The lists and full proportions, are all made

Out of his subject: and we here dispatch

You, good Cornelius, and you, Voltemand,

For bearers of this greeting to old Norway;

Giving to you no further personal power

To business with the king, more than the scope

Of these delated articles allow.

Farewell, and let your haste commend your duty[5].

CORNELIUS/VOLTEMAND: In that and all things will we show our duty.

KING CLAUDIUS: We doubt it nothing: heartily farewell.

[Exeunt VOLTEMAND and CORNELIUS]

And now, Laertes, what's the news with you?

---

[3] Disjointed

[4] Bonds

[5] Again, touching on the distant political subplot. King Claudius is dispatching his ambassadors in an attempt to stop Fortinbras.

You told us of some suit; what is't, Laertes?

You cannot speak of reason to the Dane,

And loose your voice: what wouldst thou beg, Laertes,

That shall not be my offer, not thy asking?

The head is not more native to the heart,

The hand more instrumental to the mouth,

Than is the throne of Denmark to thy father.

What wouldst thou have, Laertes?

LAERTES: My dread lord,

Your leave and favour to return to France;

From whence though willingly I came to Denmark,

To show my duty in your coronation,

Yet now, I must confess, that duty done,

My thoughts and wishes bend again toward France

And bow them to your gracious leave and pardon.

KING CLAUDIUS: Have you your father's leave? What says Polonius?

LORD POLONIUS: He hath, my lord, wrung from me my slow leave

By laboursome petition, and at last

Upon his will I seal'd my hard consent:

I do beseech you, give him leave to go.

KING CLAUDIUS: Take thy fair hour, Laertes; time be thine,

And thy best graces spend it at thy will[6]!

But now, my cousin Hamlet, and my son[7],

---

[6] "Go on and have a good time!"

[7] Again, doubling up on notes of incest, relationships muddled both for Hamlet and for his mother Gertrude

HAMLET: [Aside] A little more than kin, and less than kind[8].

KING CLAUDIUS: How is it that the clouds still hang on you?

HAMLET: Not so, my lord; I am too much i' the sun.

QUEEN GERTRUDE: Good Hamlet, cast thy nighted colour off[9],

And let thine eye look like a friend on Denmark.

Do not for ever with thy vailed lids

Seek for thy noble father in the dust:

Thou know'st 'tis common; all that lives must die,

Passing through nature to eternity.

HAMLET: Ay, madam, it is common.

QUEEN GERTRUDE: If it be,

Why seems it so particular with thee?

HAMLET: Seems, madam! nay it is; I know not 'seems.'

'Tis not alone my inky cloak, good mother,

Nor customary suits of solemn black,

Nor windy suspiration of forced breath,

No, nor the fruitful river in the eye,

Nor the dejected 'havior of the visage,

Together with all forms, moods, shapes of grief,

That can denote me truly: these indeed seem,

For they are actions that a man might play:

But I have that within which passeth show;

---

[8] Hamlet's famous first words and delicious pun, "less than kind" could refer to Claudius (as either king, or also as a being unkind) or also to Hamlet himself, he is not of Claudius' kind; ie; he is not his "son" as he has been called in the previous line

[9] The implication is that everyone else has moved beyond the period of mourning, but that Hamlet still insists on continuing to wear all black in memory of his father

These but the trappings and the suits of woe[10].

KING CLAUDIUS: 'Tis sweet and commendable in your nature, Hamlet,

To give these mourning duties to your father:

But, you must know, your father lost a father;

That father lost, lost his, and the survivor bound

In filial obligation for some term

To do obsequious sorrow: but to persever

In obstinate condolement is a course

Of impious stubbornness; 'tis unmanly grief;

It shows a will most incorrect to heaven,

A heart unfortified, a mind impatient,

An understanding simple and unschool'd:

For what we know must be and is as common

As any the most vulgar thing to sense,

Why should we in our peevish opposition

Take it to heart? Fie! 'tis a fault to heaven,

A fault against the dead, a fault to nature,

To reason most absurd: whose common theme

Is death of fathers, and who still hath cried,

From the first corse till he that died to-day,

'This must be so.' We pray you, throw to earth

This unprevailing woe, and think of us

As of a father: for let the world take note,

You are the most immediate to our throne;

And with no less nobility of love

---

[10] Gertrude is conflating a distinction between the apparent (the "seems") and the reality, thinking that Hamlet's period of extended mourning represents a conscious disruption on his part. Hamlet corrects her by asserting that he is not merely acting, but still bearing the heavy burden of his father's loss.

Than that which dearest father bears his son,

Do I impart toward you[11]. For your intent

In going back to school in Wittenberg[12],

It is most retrograde to our desire:

And we beseech you, bend you to remain

Here, in the cheer and comfort of our eye,

Our chiefest courtier, cousin, and our son.

QUEEN GERTRUDE: Let not thy mother lose her prayers, Hamlet:

I pray thee, stay with us; go not to Wittenberg.

HAMLET: I shall in all my best obey you, madam.

KING CLAUDIUS: Why, 'tis a loving and a fair reply:

Be as ourself in Denmark. Madam, come;

This gentle and unforced accord of Hamlet

Sits smiling to my heart: in grace whereof,

No jocund health that Denmark drinks to-day,

But the great cannon to the clouds shall tell,

And the king's rouse[13] the heavens all bruit again,

Re-speaking earthly thunder. Come away.

[Exeunt all but HAMLET]

HAMLET: O, that this too too solid flesh would melt

Thaw and resolve itself into a dew!

Or that the Everlasting had not fix'd

---

[11] Claudius, like Gertrude, believes that Hamlet is wallowing in his grief simply for the sake of being stubborn and "unmanly"

[12] It is understood that Hamlet was away "in school" at Wittenberg and returned upon the news of his father's death. There remains some controversy and confusion about Hamlet's exact age, and whether he was simply a college student, or an older grad student

[13] Carouse; deep plentiful drinking

His canon 'gainst self-slaughter![14] O God! God!

How weary, stale, flat and unprofitable,

Seem to me all the uses of this world!

Fie on't! ah fie! 'tis an unweeded garden,

That grows to seed; things rank and gross in nature

Possess it merely. That it should come to this!

But two months dead: nay, not so much, not two:

So excellent a king; that was, to this,

Hyperion to a satyr[15]; so loving to my mother

That he might not beteem[16] the winds of heaven

Visit her face too roughly. Heaven and earth!

Must I remember? why, she would hang on him,

As if increase of appetite had grown

By what it fed on: and yet, within a month—

Let me not think on't—Frailty, thy name is woman!

A little month, or ere those shoes were old

With which she follow'd my poor father's body,

Like Niobe, all tears:—why she, even she—

O, God! a beast, that wants discourse of reason,

Would have mourn'd longer—married with my uncle,

My father's brother, but no more like my father

Than I to Hercules: within a month:

Ere yet the salt of most unrighteous tears

Had left the flushing in her galled eyes,

---

[14] "If only my body could dissolve away. Or if only God didn't consider it a crime to kill oneself…"

[15] Hyperion - god; satyr - goat creature; Hamlet says that his father was like a god, and his uncle Claudius a short stubby goat man

[16] Allow

She married. O, most wicked speed, to post

With such dexterity to incestuous sheets!

It is not nor it cannot come to good:

But break, my heart; for I must hold my tongue.

[Enter HORATIO, MARCELLUS, and BERNARDO]

HORATIO: Hail to your lordship!

HAMLET: I am glad to see you well:

Horatio, or I do forget myself.

HORATIO: The same, my lord, and your poor servant ever.

HAMLET: Sir, my good friend; I'll change that name with you:

And what make you from Wittenberg, Horatio? Marcellus?

MARCELLUS: My good lord—

HAMLET: I am very glad to see you. Good even, sir.

But what, in faith, make you from Wittenberg?

HORATIO: A truant disposition, good my lord.

HAMLET: I would not hear your enemy say so,

Nor shall you do mine ear that violence,

To make it truster of your own report

Against yourself: I know you are no truant.

But what is your affair in Elsinore?

We'll teach you to drink deep ere you depart.

HORATIO: My lord, I came to see your father's funeral.

HAMLET: I pray thee, do not mock me, fellow-student;

I think it was to see my mother's wedding.

HORATIO: Indeed, my lord, it follow'd hard upon.

HAMLET: Thrift, thrift, Horatio! the funeral baked meats

Did coldly furnish forth the marriage tables.[17]

Would I had met my dearest foe in heaven

Or ever I had seen that day, Horatio!

My father!—methinks I see my father.

HORATIO: Where, my lord?

HAMLET: In my mind's eye, Horatio.

HORATIO: I saw him once; he was a goodly king.

HAMLET: He was a man, take him for all in all,

I shall not look upon his like again.

HORATIO: My lord, I think I saw him yesternight.

HAMLET: Saw? who?

HORATIO: My lord, the king your father.

HAMLET: The king my father!

HORATIO: Season your admiration for awhile

With an attent ear, till I may deliver,

Upon the witness of these gentlemen,

This marvel to you.

HAMLET: For God's love, let me hear.

HORATIO: Two nights together had these gentlemen,

Marcellus and Bernardo, on their watch,

In the dead vast and middle of the night,

Been thus encounter'd. A figure like your father,

Armed at point exactly, cap-a-pe,

Appears before them, and with solemn march

Goes slow and stately by them: thrice he walk'd

---

[17] A dark joke; Hamlet joking that the funeral and wedding happened in such quick succession that they were able to save money by hanging on to the funeral foods to supply the wedding feast (see Hudson)

By their oppress'd and fear-surprised eyes,

Within his truncheon's length; whilst they, distilled

Almost to jelly with the act of fear,

Stand dumb and speak not to him. This to me

In dreadful secrecy impart they did;

And I with them the third night kept the watch;

Where, as they had deliver'd, both in time,

Form of the thing, each word made true and good,

The apparition comes: I knew your father;

These hands are not more like.

HAMLET: But where was this?

MARCELLUS: My lord, upon the platform where we watch'd.

HAMLET: Did you not speak to it?

HORATIO: My lord, I did;

But answer made it none: yet once methought

It lifted up its head and did address

Itself to motion, like as it would speak;

But even then the morning cock crew loud,

And at the sound it shrunk in haste away,

And vanish'd from our sight.

HAMLET: 'Tis very strange.

HORATIO: As I do live, my honour'd lord, 'tis true;

And we did think it writ down in our duty

To let you know of it.

HAMLET: Indeed, indeed, sirs, but this troubles me.

Hold you the watch to-night?

MARCELLUS/BERNARDO: We do, my lord.

HAMLET: Arm'd, say you?

MARCELLUS/BERNARDO: Arm'd, my lord.

HAMLET: From top to toe?

MARCELLUS/BERNARDO: My lord, from head to foot.

HAMLET: Then saw you not his face?

HORATIO: O, yes, my lord; he wore his beaver[18] up.

HAMLET: What, look'd he frowningly?

HORATIO: A countenance more in sorrow than in anger.

HAMLET: Pale or red?

HORATIO: Nay, very pale.

HAMLET: And fix'd his eyes upon you?

HORATIO: Most constantly.

HAMLET: I would I had been there.

HORATIO: It would have much amazed you.

HAMLET: Very like, very like. Stay'd it long?

HORATIO: While one with moderate haste might tell a hundred.

MARCELLUS/BERNARDO: Longer, longer.

HORATIO: Not when I saw't.

HAMLET: His beard was grizzled, no?

HORATIO: It was, as I have seen it in his life,

A sable silver'd.

HAMLET: I will watch to-night;

Perchance 'twill walk again.

HORATIO: I warrant it will.

HAMLET: If it assume my noble father's person,

I'll speak to it, though hell itself should gape

And bid me hold my peace. I pray you all,

---

[18] Helmet shield

If you have hitherto conceal'd this sight,

Let it be tenable in your silence still;

And whatsoever else shall hap to-night,

Give it an understanding, but no tongue:

I will requite your loves. So, fare you well:

Upon the platform, 'twixt eleven and twelve,

I'll visit you.

ALL: Our duty to your honour.

HAMLET: Your loves, as mine to you: farewell.

[Exeunt all but HAMLET]

My father's spirit in arms! all is not well;

I doubt[19] some foul play: would the night were come!

Till then sit still, my soul: foul deeds will rise,

Though all the earth o'erwhelm them, to men's eyes.

[Exit]

---

[19] Suspect

ACT I: SCENE III

SCENE III. Polonius' house.

[Enter LAERTES and OPHELIA]

LAERTES: My necessaries are embark'd[1]: farewell:

And, sister, as the winds give benefit

And convoy is assistant, do not sleep,

But let me hear from you.

OPHELIA: Do you doubt that?

LAERTES: For Hamlet and the trifling of his favour,

Hold it a fashion and a toy in blood,

A violet in the youth of primy nature,

Forward, not permanent, sweet, not lasting,

The perfume and suppliance of a minute; No more[2].

OPHELIA: No more but so?

LAERTES: Think it no more;

For nature, crescent, does not grow alone

In thews[3] and bulk, but, as this temple waxes,

The inward service of the mind and soul

Grows wide withal. Perhaps he loves you now,

And now no soil nor cautel[4] doth besmirch

The virtue of his will: but you must fear,

His greatness weigh'd, his will is not his own;

---

[1] "My bags are packed, I'm ready to go..."

[2] What a kind brother - "Hamlet doesn't actually like you, he's just playing with you to pass the time."

[3] Muscles

[4] Caution

For he himself is subject to his birth:

He may not, as unvalued persons do,

Carve for himself; for on his choice depends

The safety and health of this whole state;

And therefore must his choice be circumscribed

Unto the voice and yielding of that body

Whereof he is the head. Then if he says he loves you,

It fits your wisdom so far to believe it

As he in his particular act and place

May give his saying deed; which is no further

Than the main voice of Denmark goes withal.

Then weigh what loss your honour may sustain,

If with too credent ear you list his songs,

Or lose your heart, or your chaste treasure open

To his unmaster'd importunity[5].

Fear it, Ophelia, fear it, my dear sister,

And keep you in the rear of your affection,

Out of the shot and danger of desire.

The chariest maid is prodigal enough,

If she unmask her beauty to the moon:

Virtue itself 'scapes not calumnious strokes:

The canker galls the infants of the spring,

Too oft before their buttons be disclosed,

And in the morn and liquid dew of youth

Contagious blastments are most imminent.

Be wary then; best safety lies in fear:

Youth to itself rebels, though none else near.

---

[5] "If you pay him too much attention back, you could lose everything."

OPHELIA: I shall the effect of this good lesson keep,

As watchman to my heart. But, good my brother,

Do not, as some ungracious pastors do,

Show me the steep and thorny way to heaven;

Whiles, like a puff'd and reckless libertine,

Himself the primrose path of dalliance treads,

And recks not his own rede[6].

LAERTES: O, fear me not.

I stay too long: but here my father comes.

[Enter POLONIUS]

A double blessing is a double grace,

Occasion smiles upon a second leave.

POLONIUS: Yet here, Laertes! aboard, aboard, for shame!

The wind sits in the shoulder of your sail,

And you are stay'd for. There; my blessing with thee!

And these few precepts in thy memory

See thou character. Give thy thoughts no tongue,

Nor any unproportioned thought his act.

Be thou familiar, but by no means vulgar.

Those friends thou hast, and their adoption tried,

Grapple them to thy soul with hoops of steel;

But do not dull thy palm with entertainment

Of each new-hatch'd, unfledged comrade. Beware

Of entrance to a quarrel, but being in,

Bear't that the opposed may beware of thee.

Give every man thy ear, but few thy voice;

---

[6] A bit of tense back and forth; Ophelia thanking him for the advice but warning him not to be a hypocrite

Take each man's censure[7], but reserve thy judgment.

Costly thy habit as thy purse can buy,

But not express'd in fancy; rich, not gaudy;

For the apparel oft proclaims the man,

And they in France of the best rank and station

Are of a most select and generous chief in that.

Neither a borrower nor a lender be;

For loan oft loses both itself and friend,

And borrowing dulls the edge of husbandry.

This above all: to thine own self be true,

And it must follow, as the night the day,

Thou canst not then be false to any man.

Farewell: my blessing season this in thee!

LAERTES: Most humbly do I take my leave, my lord.

POLONIUS: The time invites you; go; your servants tend.

LAERTES: Farewell, Ophelia; and remember well

What I have said to you.

OPHELIA: 'Tis in my memory lock'd,

And you yourself shall keep the key of it.

LAERTES: Farewell.

[Exit]

POLONIUS: What is't, Ophelia, be hath said to you?

OPHELIA: So please you, something touching the Lord Hamlet.

POLONIUS: Marry, well bethought:

'Tis told me, he hath very oft of late

Given private time to you; and you yourself

Have of your audience been most free and bounteous:

---

[7] opinion

If it be so, as so 'tis put on me,

And that in way of caution, I must tell you,

You do not understand yourself so clearly

As it behoves my daughter and your honour.

What is between you? give me up the truth.

OPHELIA: He hath, my lord, of late made many tenders

Of his affection to me.

POLONIUS: Affection! pooh! you speak like a green girl,

Unsifted[8] in such perilous circumstance.

Do you believe his tenders, as you call them?

OPHELIA: I do not know, my lord, what I should think.

POLONIUS: Marry, I'll teach you: think yourself a baby;

That you have ta'en these tenders for true pay,

Which are not sterling[9]. Tender yourself more dearly;

Or—not to crack the wind of the poor phrase,

Running it thus—you'll tender me a fool.

OPHELIA: My lord, he hath importuned me with love

In honourable fashion.

POLONIUS: Ay, fashion you may call it; go to, go to.

OPHELIA: And hath given countenance to his speech, my lord,

With almost all the holy vows of heaven.

POLONIUS: Ay, springes to catch woodcocks. I do know,

When the blood burns, how prodigal the soul

Lends the tongue vows: these blazes, daughter,

Giving more light than heat, extinct in both,

---

[8] Untested

[9] An extended money metaphor - "You are interpreting Hamlet's attention as favors representing the true currency of love, but it is inaccurate to do this."

Even in their promise, as it is a-making,

You must not take for fire. From this time

Be somewhat scanter of your maiden presence;

Set your entreatments at a higher rate

Than a command to parley. For Lord Hamlet,

Believe so much in him, that he is young

And with a larger tether may he walk

Than may be given you: in few, Ophelia,

Do not believe his vows; for they are brokers[10],

Not of that dye which their investments show,

But mere implorators of unholy suits,

Breathing like sanctified and pious bawds,

The better to beguile. This is for all:

I would not, in plain terms, from this time forth,

Have you so slander any moment leisure,

As to give words or talk with the Lord Hamlet.

Look to't, I charge you: come your ways.

OPHELIA: I shall obey, my lord.

[Exeunt]

---

[10] temporary

ACT I: SCENE IV

SCENE IV. Elsinore Castle - The Guard Platform

[Enter HAMLET, HORATIO, and MARCELLUS]

HAMLET: The air bites shrewdly; it is very cold.

HORATIO: It is a nipping and an eager air.

HAMLET: What hour now?

HORATIO: I think it lacks of twelve.

HAMLET: No, it is struck.

HORATIO: Indeed? I heard it not: then it draws near the season

Wherein the spirit held his wont to walk.

A flourish of trumpets, and ordnance shot off, within

What does this mean, my lord?

HAMLET: The king doth wake to-night and takes his rouse,

Keeps wassail, and the swaggering up-spring reels;

And, as he drains his draughts of Rhenish down,

The kettle-drum and trumpet thus bray out

The triumph of his pledge.

HORATIO: Is it a custom?

HAMLET: Ay, marry, is't:

But to my mind, though I am native here

And to the manner born, it is a custom

More honour'd in the breach than the observance[1].

This heavy-headed revel east and west

---

[1] This exchange is meant to underscore how different Claudius is when compared to the former King Hamlet; Claudius riotously indulges in the wild drinking and partying that the Danes are known for, but it would actually be more honorable to abandon such a tradition

Makes us traduced and tax'd of other nations:

They clepe[2] us drunkards, and with swinish phrase

Soil our addition; and indeed it takes

From our achievements, though perform'd at height,

The pith and marrow of our attribute.

So, oft it chances in particular men,

That for some vicious mole of nature in them,

As, in their birth—wherein they are not guilty,

Since nature cannot choose his origin—

By the o'ergrowth of some complexion,

Oft breaking down the pales and forts of reason,

Or by some habit that too much o'er-leavens

The form of plausive manners, that these men,

Carrying, I say, the stamp of one defect,

Being nature's livery, or fortune's star,

Their virtues else—be they as pure as grace,

As infinite as man may undergo—

Shall in the general censure take corruption

From that particular fault: the dram of eale

Doth all the noble substance of a doubt

To his own scandal.

HORATIO: Look, my lord, it comes!

[Enter Ghost]

HAMLET: Angels and ministers of grace defend us!

Be thou a spirit of health or goblin damn'd,

Bring with thee airs from heaven or blasts from hell,

Be thy intents wicked or charitable,

---

2 Call

Thou comest in such a questionable shape

That I will speak to thee: I'll call thee Hamlet,

King, father, royal Dane: O, answer me!

Let me not burst in ignorance; but tell

Why thy canonized bones, hearsed in death,

Have burst their cerements[3]; why the sepulchre,

Wherein we saw thee quietly inurn'd,

Hath oped his ponderous and marble jaws,

To cast thee up again. What may this mean,

That thou, dead corse, again in complete steel

Revisit'st thus the glimpses of the moon,

Making night hideous; and we fools of nature

So horridly to shake our disposition

With thoughts beyond the reaches of our souls?

Say, why is this? wherefore[4]? what should we do?

[Ghost beckons HAMLET]

HORATIO: It beckons you to go away with it,

As if it some impartment did desire

To you alone.

MARCELLUS: Look, with what courteous action

It waves you to a more removed ground:

But do not go with it.

HORATIO: No, by no means.

HAMLET: It will not speak; then I will follow it.

HORATIO: Do not, my lord.

HAMLET: Why, what should be the fear?

---

[3] Burst from their coffins

[4] For Shakespeare, wherefore = why

I do not set my life in a pin's fee;

And for my soul, what can it do to that,

Being a thing immortal as itself?

It waves me forth again: I'll follow it.

HORATIO: What if it tempt you toward the flood, my lord,

Or to the dreadful summit of the cliff

That beetles o'er his base into the sea,

And there assume some other horrible form,

Which might deprive your sovereignty of reason

And draw you into madness? think of it:

The very place puts toys of desperation,

Without more motive, into every brain

That looks so many fathoms to the sea

And hears it roar beneath.

HAMLET: It waves me still.

Go on; I'll follow thee.

MARCELLUS: You shall not go, my lord.

HAMLET: Hold off your hands.

HORATIO: Be ruled; you shall not go.

HAMLET: My fate cries out,

And makes each petty artery in this body

As hardy as the Nemean lion's nerve.

Still am I call'd. Unhand me, gentlemen.

By heaven, I'll make a ghost of him that lets[5] me!

I say, away! Go on; I'll follow thee.

[Exeunt Ghost and HAMLET]

HORATIO: He waxes desperate with imagination.

---

[5] Tries to stop

MARCELLUS: Let's follow; 'tis not fit thus to obey him.

HORATIO: Have after. To what issue will this come?

MARCELLUS: Something is rotten in the state of Denmark.

HORATIO: Heaven will direct it.

MARCELLUS: Nay, let's follow him.

[Exeunt]

ACT I: SCENE V

SCENE V. Another part of the platform.

[Enter GHOST and HAMLET]

HAMLET: Where wilt thou lead me? speak; I'll go no further.

GHOST: Mark me.

HAMLET: I will.

GHOST: My hour is almost come,

When I to sulphurous and tormenting flames

Must render up myself[1].

HAMLET: Alas, poor ghost!

GHOST: Pity me not, but lend thy serious hearing

To what I shall unfold.

HAMLET: Speak; I am bound to hear.

GHOST: So art thou to revenge, when thou shalt hear.

HAMLET: What?

GHOST: I am thy father's spirit,

Doom'd for a certain term to walk the night,

And for the day confined to fast in fires,

Till the foul crimes done in my days of nature

Are burnt and purged away. But that I am forbid

To tell the secrets of my prison-house,

I could a tale unfold whose lightest word

Would harrow up thy soul, freeze thy young blood,

Make thy two eyes, like stars, start from their spheres,

Thy knotted and combined locks to part

---

[1] The ghost is saying that the soul of Hamlet's father resides in purgatory

And each particular hair to stand on end,

Like quills upon the fretful porpentine[2]:

But this eternal blazon must not be

To ears of flesh and blood. List, list, O, list![3]

If thou didst ever thy dear father love—

HAMLET: O God!

GHOST: Revenge his foul and most unnatural murder.

HAMLET: Murder!

GHOST: Murder most foul, as in the best it is;

But this most foul, strange and unnatural.

HAMLET: Haste me to know't, that I, with wings as swift

As meditation or the thoughts of love,

May sweep to my revenge.

GHOST: I find thee apt;

And duller shouldst thou be than the fat weed

That roots itself in ease on Lethe wharf,

Wouldst thou not stir in this. Now, Hamlet, hear:

'Tis given out that, sleeping in my orchard,

A serpent stung me; so the whole ear of Denmark

Is by a forged process of my death

Rankly abused: but know, thou noble youth,

The serpent that did sting thy father's life

Now wears his crown.

HAMLET: O my prophetic soul! My uncle!

GHOST: Ay, that incestuous, that adulterate beast,

With witchcraft of his wit, with traitorous gifts,—

---

2 Porcupine

3 Listen

O wicked wit and gifts, that have the power

So to seduce!—won to his shameful lust

The will of my most seeming-virtuous queen:

O Hamlet, what a falling-off was there!

From me, whose love was of that dignity

That it went hand in hand even with the vow

I made to her in marriage, and to decline

Upon a wretch whose natural gifts were poor

To[4] those of mine!

But virtue, as it never will be moved,

Though lewdness court it in a shape of heaven,

So lust, though to a radiant angel link'd,

Will sate itself in a celestial bed,

And prey on garbage.

But, soft! methinks I scent the morning air;

Brief let me be. Sleeping within my orchard,

My custom always of the afternoon,

Upon my secure hour thy uncle stole,

With juice of cursed hebenon in a vial,

And in the porches of my ears did pour

The leperous distilment; whose effect

Holds such an enmity with blood of man

That swift as quicksilver it courses through

The natural gates and alleys of the body,

And with a sudden vigour doth posset

And curd, like eager droppings into milk,

The thin and wholesome blood: so did it mine;

---

[4] Compared to

And a most instant tetter bark'd about,

Most lazar-like, with vile and loathsome crust,

All my smooth body.

Thus was I, sleeping, by a brother's hand

Of life, of crown, of queen, at once dispatch'd:

Cut off even in the blossoms of my sin[5],

Unhousel'd, disappointed, unanel'd,

No reckoning made, but sent to my account

With all my imperfections on my head:

O, horrible! O, horrible! most horrible!

If thou hast nature[6] in thee, bear it not;

Let not the royal bed of Denmark be

A couch for luxury and damned incest.

But, howsoever thou pursuest this act,

Taint not thy mind, nor let thy soul contrive

Against thy mother aught: leave her to heaven

And to those thorns that in her bosom lodge,

To prick and sting her. Fare thee well at once!

The glow-worm shows the matin[7] to be near,

And 'gins to pale his uneffectual fire:

Adieu, adieu! Hamlet, remember me.

[Exit]

HAMLET: O all you host of heaven! O earth! what else?

And shall I couple hell? O, fie! Hold, hold, my heart;

And you, my sinews, grow not instant old,

---

[5] Without even having had the chance to confess my sins and receive absolution

[6] Natural affection (Hudson)

[7] Morning

But bear me stiffly up. Remember thee!

Ay, thou poor ghost, while memory holds a seat

In this distracted globe[8]. Remember thee!

Yea, from the table[9] of my memory

I'll wipe away all trivial fond records,

All saws of books, all forms, all pressures past,

That youth and observation copied there;

And thy commandment all alone shall live

Within the book and volume of my brain,

Unmix'd with baser matter: yes, by heaven!

O most pernicious woman!

O villain, villain, smiling, damned villain!

My tables, meet it is I set it down,

That one may smile, and smile, and be a villain;

At least I'm sure it may be so in Denmark:

So, uncle, there you are. Now to my word;

It is 'Adieu, adieu! remember me.'

I have sworn 't.

MARCELLUS/HORATIO: [Within] My lord, my lord—

MARCELLUS: [Within] Lord Hamlet—

HORATIO: [Within] Heaven secure him!

HAMLET: So be it!

HORATIO: [Within] Hillo, ho, ho, my lord!

HAMLET: Hillo, ho, ho, boy! come, bird, come.

[Enter HORATIO and MARCELLUS]

---

[8] Head

[9] Tablet

MARCELLUS: How is't, my noble lord?

HORATIO: What news, my lord?

HAMLET: O, wonderful!

HORATIO: Good my lord, tell it.

HAMLET: No; you'll reveal it.

HORATIO: Not I, my lord, by heaven.

MARCELLUS: Nor I, my lord.

HAMLET: How say you, then; would heart of man once think it?

But you'll be secret?

HORATIO/MARCELLUS: Ay, by heaven, my lord.

HAMLET: There's ne'er a villain dwelling in all Denmark

But he's an arrant knave.

HORATIO: There needs no ghost, my lord, come from the grave

To tell us this.

HAMLET: Why, right; you are i' the right;

And so, without more circumstance at all,

I hold it fit that we shake hands and part:

You, as your business and desire shall point you;

For every man has business and desire,

Such as it is; and for mine own poor part,

Look you, I'll go pray.

HORATIO: These are but wild and whirling words, my lord.

HAMLET: I'm sorry they offend you, heartily;

Yes, 'faith heartily.

HORATIO: There's no offence, my lord.

HAMLET: Yes, by Saint Patrick, but there is, Horatio,

And much offence too. Touching this vision here,

It is an honest ghost, that let me tell you:

For your desire to know what is between us,

O'ermaster 't as you may. And now, good friends,

As you are friends, scholars and soldiers,

Give me one poor request.

HORATIO: What is't, my lord? we will.

HAMLET: Never make known what you have seen to-night.

HORATIO/MARCELLUS: My lord, we will not.

HAMLET: Nay, but swear't.

HORATIO: In faith,

My lord, not I.

MARCELLUS: Nor I, my lord, in faith.

HAMLET: Upon my sword.

MARCELLUS: We have sworn, my lord, already.

HAMLET: Indeed, upon my sword, indeed.

GHOST: [Beneath] Swear.

HAMLET: Ah, ha, boy! say'st thou so? art thou there, truepenny[10]?

Come on—you hear this fellow in the cellarage—

Consent to swear.

HORATIO: Propose the oath, my lord.

HAMLET: Never to speak of this that you have seen,

Swear by my sword.

GHOST: [Beneath] Swear.

HAMLET: Hic et ubique[11]? then we'll shift our ground.

Come hither, gentlemen,

---

[10] Old version of "My good honest man"

[11] Latin for "here and everywhere"

And lay your hands again upon my sword:

Never to speak of this that you have heard,

Swear by my sword.

GHOST: [Beneath] Swear.

HAMLET: Well said, old mole! canst work i' the earth so fast?

A worthy pioneer! Once more remove, good friends.

HORATIO: O day and night, but this is wondrous strange!

HAMLET: And therefore as a stranger give it welcome.

There are more things in heaven and earth, Horatio,

Than are dreamt of in your philosophy. But come;

Here, as before, never, so help you mercy,

How strange or odd soe'er[12] I bear myself,

As I perchance hereafter shall think meet

To put an antic disposition on,

That you, at such times seeing me, never shall,

With arms encumber'd thus, or this headshake,

Or by pronouncing of some doubtful phrase,

As 'Well, well, we know,' or 'We could, an if we would,'

Or 'If we list to speak,' or 'There be, an if they might,'

Or such ambiguous giving out, to note

That you know aught of me: this not to do,

So grace and mercy at your most need help you, Swear.

GHOST: [Beneath] Swear.

HAMLET: Rest, rest, perturbed spirit!

They swear

So, gentlemen,

With all my love I do commend me to you:

---

[12] so ever

And what so poor a man as Hamlet is

May do, to express his love and friending to you,

God willing, shall not lack. Let us go in together;

And still your fingers on your lips, I pray.

The time is out of joint: O cursed spite,

That ever I was born to set it right!

Nay, come, let's go together.

[Exeunt]

ACT I ASSESSMENT

The first act in Hamlet does a masterful job of laying out the stakes and ends with a flourish in the form of a visit from the ghost. Additionally, it presents a cliffhanger ending in the form of Hamlet's father telling him that he was murdered and that his death needs to be avenged. Hamlet quickly devises his plan to "put on an antic disposition" - that is, to pretend to be mentally disturbed as the first part of his plot to avenge his father. (More on this later).

By now, the stakes have been well established. We are invested in the woes of our main character (expressed through lengthy soliloquies that reveal his inner thoughts) and we sympathize with his plight. Smaller characters such as Polonius, Ophelia, and Laertes have been given proper introductions and we know to look out for them and their contributions later in the story.

All in all, one of Shakespeare's most powerful plays is off to a momentous start!

ACT II SUMMARY

Act II begins much in the same flavor as Act I ended—Polonius meets with his servant Reynaldo and sends him along to keep an eye on his son Laertes during his travels. From there, Polonius meets again with his daughter Ophelia. Ophelia tells her father that Hamlet came to visit her and that he's been acting strangely. Polonius listens to her words but then reiterates his warning to avoid Hamlet's so-called "affections."

From there, we join the King and Queen. Polonius relays his observations to Claudius and Gertrude, and they begin to wonder about Hamlet's sanity. When Hamlet arrives, Polonius attempts to engage him in conversation, only to be confused by Hamlet's nonsensical replies.

Later, two of Hamlet's classmates, Rosencrantz and Guildenstern, arrive in Denmark. We learn that King Claudius invited them in the hopes that they might be able to do a bit of spying on Hamlet and figure out why he's been acting to strange lately.

Lastly, a traveling group of actors arrive at the castle and entertain Hamlet by reciting a series of monologues. From there, Hamlet comes up with an idea to have them perform a play that discusses themes of regicide and murder. He hopes that through spying on his uncle during this performance he may be able to "catch the conscience of the king" and thereby gain proof that his uncle did indeed murder his father.

ACT II: SCENE I

SCENE I. A room in POLONIUS' house.

[Enter POLONIUS and REYNALDO]

POLONIUS: Give him this money and these notes, Reynaldo.

REYNALDO: I will, my lord.

POLONIUS: You shall do marvelous wisely, good Reynaldo,

Before you visit him, to make inquire

Of his behavior.

REYNALDO: My lord, I did intend it.

POLONIUS: Marry, well said; very well said. Look you, sir,

Inquire me first what Danskers are in Paris;

And how, and who, what means, and where they keep[1],

What company, at what expense; and finding

By this encompassment and drift of question

That they do know my son, come you more nearer

Than your particular demands will touch it:

Take you, as 'twere, some distant knowledge of him;

As thus, 'I know his father and his friends,

And in part him: ' do you mark this, Reynaldo?

REYNALDO: Ay, very well, my lord.

POLONIUS: 'And in part him; but' you may say 'not well:

But, if't be he I mean, he's very wild;

Addicted so and so:' and there put on him

What forgeries you please; marry, none so rank

---

[1] live

As may dishonour him; take heed of that;

But, sir, such wanton, wild and usual slips

As are companions noted and most known

To youth and liberty.

REYNALDO: As gaming, my lord.

POLONIUS: Ay, or drinking, fencing, swearing, quarrelling,

Drabbing: you may go so far.

REYNALDO: My lord, that would dishonour him.

POLONIUS: 'Faith, no; as you may season it in the charge

You must not put another scandal on him,

That he is open to incontinency;

That's not my meaning: but breathe his faults so quaintly

That they may seem the taints of liberty,

The flash and outbreak of a fiery mind,

A savageness in unreclaimed blood,

Of general assault.

REYNALDO: But, my good lord—

POLONIUS: Wherefore should you do this?

REYNALDO: Ay, my lord,

I would know that.

POLONIUS: Marry, sir, here's my drift;

And I believe, it is a fetch of wit:

You laying these slight sullies on my son,

As 'twere a thing a little soil'd i' the working, Mark you,

Your party in converse, him you would sound,

Having ever seen in the prenominate crimes

The youth you breathe of guilty, be assured

He closes with you in this consequence;

'Good sir,' or so, or 'friend,' or 'gentleman,'

According to the phrase or the addition

Of man and country.

REYNALDO: Very good, my lord.

POLONIUS: And then, sir, does he this—he does—what was I

about to say? By the mass, I was about to say

something: where did I leave?

REYNALDO: At 'closes in the consequence,' at 'friend or so,'

and 'gentleman.'

POLONIUS: At 'closes in the consequence,' ay, marry;

He closes thus: 'I know the gentleman;

I saw him yesterday, or t' other day,

Or then, or then; with such, or such; and, as you say,

There was a' gaming; there o'ertook in's rouse;

There falling out at tennis:' or perchance,

'I saw him enter such a house of sale,'

Videlicet, a brothel, or so forth.

See you now;

Your bait of falsehood takes this carp of truth:

And thus do we of wisdom and of reach,

With windlasses and with assays of bias,

By indirections find directions out:

So by my former lecture and advice,

Shall you my son. You have me, have you not?

REYNALDO: My lord, I have.

POLONIUS: God be wi' you; fare you well.

REYNALDO: Good my lord!

POLONIUS: Observe his inclination in yourself.

REYNALDO: I shall, my lord.

POLONIUS: And let him ply his music.

REYNALDO: Well, my lord.

POLONIUS: Farewell!

[Exit REYNALDO]

[Enter OPHELIA]

How now, Ophelia! what's the matter?

OPHELIA: O, my lord, my lord, I have been so affrighted!

POLONIUS: With what, i' the name of God?

OPHELIA: My lord, as I was sewing in my closet,

Lord Hamlet, with his doublet all unbraced[2];

No hat upon his head; his stockings foul'd,

Ungarter'd, and down-gyved to his ankle;

Pale as his shirt; his knees knocking each other;

And with a look so piteous in purport

As if he had been loosed out of hell

To speak of horrors,—he comes before me.

POLONIUS: Mad for thy love?

OPHELIA: My lord, I do not know;

But truly, I do fear it.

POLONIUS: What said he?

OPHELIA: He took me by the wrist and held me hard;

Then goes he to the length of all his arm;

And, with his other hand thus o'er his brow,

He falls to such perusal of my face

As he would draw it. Long stay'd he so;

---

[2] unbuttoned

At last, a little shaking of mine arm

And thrice his head thus waving up and down,

He raised a sigh so piteous and profound

As it did seem to shatter all his bulk

And end his being: that done, he lets me go:

And, with his head over his shoulder turn'd,

He seem'd to find his way without his eyes;

For out o' doors he went without their helps,

And, to the last, bended their light on me.

POLONIUS: Come, go with me: I will go seek the king.

This is the very ecstasy of love,

Whose violent property fordoes itself

And leads the will to desperate undertakings

As oft as any passion under heaven

That does afflict our natures. I am sorry.

What, have you given him any hard words of late?

OPHELIA: No, my good lord, but, as you did command,

I did repel his fetters and denied

His access to me.

POLONIUS: That hath made him mad.

I am sorry that with better heed and judgment

I had not quoted[3] him: I fear'd he did but trifle,

And meant to wreck thee; but, beshrew my jealousy[4]!

By heaven, it is as proper to our age

To cast beyond ourselves in our opinions

As it is common for the younger sort

---

[3] observed

[4] "Beshrew" for "Confound it!" (Hudson)

To lack discretion. Come, go we to the king:

This must be known; which, being kept close, might move

More grief to hide than hate to utter love.

Come.

[Exeunt]

ACT II: SCENE II

SCENE II. A room in the castle.

[Enter KING CLAUDIUS, QUEEN GERTRUDE, ROSENCRANTZ, GUILDENSTERN, and Attendants]

KING CLAUDIUS: Welcome, dear Rosencrantz and Guildenstern!

Moreover that[1] we much did long to see you,

The need we have to use you did provoke

Our hasty sending. Something have you heard

Of Hamlet's transformation; so call it,

Sith nor the exterior nor the inward man

Resembles that it was. What it should be,

More than his father's death, that thus hath put him

So much from the understanding of himself,

I cannot dream of: I entreat you both,

That, being of so young days brought up with him,

And sith so neighbour'd to his youth and havior[2],

That you vouchsafe your rest here in our court

Some little time: so by your companies

To draw him on to pleasures, and to gather,

So much as from occasion you may glean,

Whether aught, to us unknown, afflicts him thus,

That, open'd, lies within our remedy.

QUEEN GERTRUDE: Good gentlemen, he hath much talk'd of you;

---

[1] "Other than the fact that…"

[2] "Since you are so familiar with his age and behavior…"

And sure I am two men there are not living

To whom he more adheres. If it will please you

To show us so much gentry and good will

As to expend your time with us awhile,

For the supply and profit of our hope,

Your visitation shall receive such thanks

As fits a king's remembrance.

ROSENCRANTZ: Both your majesties

Might, by the sovereign power you have of us,

Put your dread pleasures more into command

Than to entreaty.

GUILDENSTERN: But we both obey,

And here give up ourselves, in the full bent

To lay our service freely at your feet,

To be commanded.

KING CLAUDIUS: Thanks, Rosencrantz and gentle Guildenstern.

QUEEN GERTRUDE: Thanks, Guildenstern and gentle Rosencrantz:

And I beseech you instantly to visit

My too much changed son. Go, some of you,

And bring these gentlemen where Hamlet is.

GUILDENSTERN: Heavens make our presence and our practises

Pleasant and helpful to him!

QUEEN GERTRUDE: Ay, amen!

[Exeunt ROSENCRANTZ, GUILDENSTERN, and some Attendants

Enter POLONIUS]

POLONIUS: The ambassadors from Norway, my good lord,

Are joyfully return'd.

KING CLAUDIUS: Thou still hast been the father of good news.

POLONIUS: Have I, my lord? I assure my good liege,

    I hold my duty, as I hold my soul,

    Both to my God and to my gracious king:

    And I do think, or else this brain of mine

    Hunts not the trail of policy so sure

    As it hath used to do, that I have found

    The very cause of Hamlet's lunacy.

KING CLAUDIUS: O, speak of that; that do I long to hear.

POLONIUS: Give first admittance to the ambassadors;

    My news shall be the fruit to that great feast.

KING CLAUDIUS: Thyself do grace to them, and bring them in.

                                        [Exit POLONIUS]

    He tells me, my dear Gertrude, he hath found

    The head and source of all your son's distemper.

QUEEN GERTRUDE: I doubt it is no other but the main;

    His father's death, and our o'erhasty marriage.

KING CLAUDIUS: Well, we shall sift him.

        [Re-enter POLONIUS, with VOLTEMAND and CORNELIUS]

    Welcome, my good friends!

    Say, Voltemand, what from our brother Norway?

VOLTEMAND: Most fair return of greetings and desires.

    Upon our first, he sent out to suppress

    His nephew's levies; which to him appear'd

    To be a preparation 'gainst the Polack;

    But, better look'd into, he truly found

    It was against your highness: whereat grieved,

    That so his sickness, age and impotence

    Was falsely borne in hand, sends out arrests

On Fortinbras; which he, in brief, obeys;

Receives rebuke from Norway, and in fine

Makes vow before his uncle never more

To give the assay of arms against your majesty.

Whereon old Norway, overcome with joy,

Gives him three thousand crowns in annual fee,

And his commission to employ those soldiers,

So levied as before, against the Polack:

With an entreaty, herein further shown,

That it might please you to give quiet pass

Through your dominions for this enterprise,

On such regards of safety and allowance

As therein are set down.

KING CLAUDIUS: It likes us well;

And at our more consider'd time well read,

Answer, and think upon this business.

Meantime we thank you for your well-took labour:

Go to your rest; at night we'll feast together:

Most welcome home!

[Exeunt VOLTEMAND and CORNELIUS]

POLONIUS: This business is well ended.

My liege, and madam, to expostulate[3]

What majesty should be, what duty is,

Why day is day, night night, and time is time,

Were nothing but to waste night, day and time.

Therefore, since brevity is the soul of wit,

---

[3] discuss

And tediousness the limbs and outward flourishes,

I will be brief: your noble son is mad:

Mad call I it; for, to define true madness,

What is't but to be nothing else but mad?

But let that go.

QUEEN GERTRUDE: More matter, with less art.

POLONIUS: Madam, I swear I use no art at all.

That he is mad, 'tis true: 'tis true 'tis pity;

And pity 'tis 'tis true: a foolish figure;

But farewell it, for I will use no art.

Mad let us grant him, then: and now remains

That we find out the cause of this effect,

Or rather say, the cause of this defect,

For this effect defective comes by cause:

Thus it remains, and the remainder thus. Perpend.

I have a daughter—have while she is mine—

Who, in her duty and obedience, mark,

Hath given me this: now gather, and surmise.

[Reads] 'To the celestial and my soul's idol, the most

beautified Ophelia,'—

That's an ill phrase, a vile phrase; 'beautified' is

a vile phrase: but you shall hear. Thus:

[Reads] 'In her excellent white bosom, these, etc.'

QUEEN GERTRUDE: Came this from Hamlet to her?

POLONIUS: Good madam, stay awhile; I will be faithful.

[Reads]

'Doubt thou the stars are fire;

Doubt that the sun doth move;

Doubt truth to be a liar;

But never doubt I love.

'O dear Ophelia, I am ill at these numbers;

I have not art to reckon my groans: but that

I love thee best, O most best, believe it. Adieu.

'Thine evermore most dear lady, whilst

this machine is to him, Hamlet.'

This, in obedience, hath my daughter shown me,

And more above, hath his solicitings,

As they fell out by time, by means and place,

All given to mine ear.

KING CLAUDIUS: But how hath she

Received his love?

POLONIUS: What do you think of me?

KING CLAUDIUS: As of a man faithful and honourable.

POLONIUS: I would fain prove so. But what might you think,

When I had seen this hot love on the wing—

As I perceived it, I must tell you that,

Before my daughter told me—what might you,

Or my dear majesty your queen here, think,

If I had play'd the desk or table-book,

Or given my heart a winking, mute and dumb,

Or look'd upon this love with idle sight;

What might you think? No, I went round to work,

And my young mistress thus I did bespeak:

'Lord Hamlet is a prince, out of thy star[4];

This must not be:' and then I precepts gave her,

---

[4] That is, beyond your station. Not meant to be.

That she should lock herself from his resort,

Admit no messengers, receive no tokens.

Which done, she took the fruits of my advice;

And he, repulsed—a short tale to make—

Fell into a sadness, then into a fast,

Thence to a watch, thence into a weakness,

Thence to a lightness, and, by this declension[5],

Into the madness wherein now he raves,

And all we mourn for.

KING CLAUDIUS: Do you think 'tis this?

QUEEN GERTRUDE: It may be, very likely.

POLONIUS: Hath there been such a time—I'd fain know that—

That I have positively said 'Tis so,'

When it proved otherwise?

KING CLAUDIUS: Not that I know.

POLONIUS: [Pointing to his head and shoulder]

Take this from this, if this be otherwise:

If circumstances lead me, I will find

Where truth is hid, though it were hid indeed

Within the centre.

KING CLAUDIUS: How may we try it further?

POLONIUS: You know, sometimes he walks four hours together

Here in the lobby.

QUEEN GERTRUDE: So he does indeed.

LORD POLONIUS: At such a time I'll loose my daughter to him:

Be you and I behind an arras then;

Mark the encounter: if he love her not

---

[5] Natural progression

And be not from his reason fall'n thereon,

Let me be no assistant for a state,

But keep a farm and carters.

KING CLAUDIUS: We will try it.

QUEEN GERTRUDE: But, look, where sadly the poor wretch comes reading.

POLONIUS: Away, I do beseech you, both away:

I'll board[6] him presently.

[Exeunt KING CLAUDIUS, QUEEN GERTRUDE, and Attendants
Enter HAMLET, reading]

O, give me leave:

How does my good Lord Hamlet?

HAMLET: Well, God-a-mercy.

POLONIUS: Do you know me, my lord?

HAMLET: Excellent well; you are a fishmonger.

POLONIUS: Not I, my lord.

HAMLET: Then I would you were so honest a man.

POLONIUS: Honest, my lord!

HAMLET: Ay, sir; to be honest, as this world goes, is to be

one man picked out of ten thousand.

POLONIUS: That's very true, my lord.

HAMLET: For if the sun breed maggots in a dead dog, being a

god kissing carrion—Have you a daughter?

POLONIUS: I have, my lord.

HAMLET: Let her not walk i' the sun: conception is a

---

[6] talk to

blessing: but not as your daughter may conceive.

Friend, look to 't.

POLONIUS: [Aside] How say you by that? Still harping on my

daughter: yet he knew me not at first; he said I

was a fishmonger: he is far gone, far gone: and

truly in my youth I suffered much extremity for

love; very near this. I'll speak to him again.

What do you read, my lord?

HAMLET: Words, words, words.

POLONIUS: What is the matter, my lord?

HAMLET: Between who?

POLONIUS: I mean, the matter that you read, my lord.

HAMLET: Slanders, sir: for the satirical rogue says here

that old men have grey beards, that their faces are

wrinkled, their eyes purging thick amber and

plum-tree gum and that they have a plentiful lack of

wit, together with most weak hams: all which, sir,

though I most powerfully and potently believe, yet

I hold it not honesty to have it thus set down, for

yourself, sir, should be old as I am, if like a crab

you could go backward.

POLONIUS: [Aside] Though this be madness, yet there is method

in 't. Will you walk out of the air, my lord?

HAMLET: Into my grave.

POLONIUS: Indeed, that is out o' the air.

[Aside] How pregnant[7] sometimes his replies are! a happiness

that often madness hits on, which reason and sanity

---

[7] Strangely thoughtful; particularly for a man losing his wits

could not so prosperously be delivered of. I will

leave him, and suddenly contrive the means of

meeting between him and my daughter.—My honourable

lord, I will most humbly take my leave of you.

HAMLET: You cannot, sir, take from me any thing that I will

more willingly part withal: except my life, except

my life, except my life.

POLONIUS: Fare you well, my lord.

HAMLET: These tedious old fools!

[Enter ROSENCRANTZ and GUILDENSTERN]

POLONIUS: You go to seek the Lord Hamlet; there he is.

ROSENCRANTZ: [To POLONIUS] God save you, sir!

[Exit POLONIUS]

GUILDENSTERN: My honoured lord!

ROSENCRANTZ: My most dear lord!

HAMLET: My excellent good friends! How dost thou,

Guildenstern? Ah, Rosencrantz! Good lads, how do ye both?

ROSENCRANTZ: As the indifferent[8] children of the earth.

GUILDENSTERN: Happy, in that we are not over-happy;

On fortune's cap we are not the very button.

HAMLET: Nor the soles of her shoe?

ROSENCRANTZ: Neither, my lord.

HAMLET: Then you live about her waist, or in the middle of

her favours?

---

[8] carefree

GUILDENSTERN: 'Faith, her privates we[9].

HAMLET: In the secret parts of fortune? O, most true; she

is a strumpet. What's the news?

ROSENCRANTZ: None, my lord, but that the world's grown honest.

HAMLET: Then is doomsday near: but your news is not true.

Let me question more in particular: what have you,

my good friends, deserved at the hands of fortune,

that she sends you to prison hither?

GUILDENSTERN: Prison, my lord!

HAMLET: Denmark's a prison.

ROSENCRANTZ: Then is the world one.

HAMLET: A goodly one; in which there are many confines,

wards and dungeons, Denmark being one o' the worst.

ROSENCRANTZ: We think not so, my lord.

HAMLET: Why, then, 'tis none to you; for there is nothing

either good or bad, but thinking makes it so: to me

it is a prison.

ROSENCRANTZ: Why then, your ambition makes it one; 'tis too

narrow for your mind.

HAMLET: O God, I could be bounded in a nut shell and count

myself a king of infinite space, were it not that I

have bad dreams.

GUILDENSTERN: Which dreams indeed are ambition, for the very

substance of the ambitious is merely the shadow of a dream.

HAMLET: A dream itself is but a shadow.

ROSENCRANTZ: Truly, and I hold ambition of so airy and light a

---

[9] Yes, an immature joke

quality that it is but a shadow's shadow.

HAMLET: Then are our beggars bodies, and our monarchs and

outstretched heroes the beggars' shadows. Shall we

to the court? for, by my fay, I cannot reason.

ROSENCRANTZ/GUILDENSTERN: We'll wait upon you.

HAMLET: No such matter: I will not sort you with the rest

of my servants, for, to speak to you like an honest

man, I am most dreadfully attended. But, in the

beaten way of friendship, what make you at Elsinore?

ROSENCRANTZ: To visit you, my lord; no other occasion.

HAMLET: Beggar that I am, I am even poor in thanks; but I

thank you: and sure, dear friends, my thanks are

too dear a halfpenny. Were you not sent for? Is it

your own inclining? Is it a free visitation? Come,

deal justly with me: come, come; nay, speak.

GUILDENSTERN: What should we say, my lord?

HAMLET: Why, any thing, but to the purpose. You were sent

for; and there is a kind of confession in your looks

which your modesties have not craft enough to colour:

I know the good king and queen have sent for you.

ROSENCRANTZ: To what end, my lord?

HAMLET: That you must teach me. But let me conjure you, by

the rights of our fellowship, by the consonancy of

our youth, by the obligation of our ever-preserved

love, and by what more dear a better proposer could

charge you withal, be even and direct with me,

whether you were sent for, or no?

ROSENCRANTZ: [Aside to GUILDENSTERN] What say you?

HAMLET: [Aside] Nay, then, I have an eye of[10] you. If you love me, hold not off.

GUILDENSTERN: My lord, we were sent for.

HAMLET: I will tell you why; so shall my anticipation prevent your discovery, and your secrecy to the king and queen moult no feather. I have of late—but wherefore I know not—lost all my mirth, forgone all custom of exercises; and indeed it goes so heavily with my disposition that this goodly frame, the earth, seems to me a sterile promontory, this most excellent canopy, the air, look you, this brave o'erhanging firmament, this majestical roof fretted with golden fire, why, it appears no other thing to me than a foul and pestilent congregation of vapours. What a piece of work is a man! how noble in reason! how infinite in faculty! in form and moving how express and admirable! in action how like an angel! in apprehension how like a god! the beauty of the world! the paragon of animals! And yet, to me, what is this quintessence of dust? man delights not me: no, nor woman neither, though by your smiling you seem to say so.

ROSENCRANTZ: My lord, there was no such stuff in my thoughts.

HAMLET: Why did you laugh then, when I said 'man delights not me'?

ROSENCRANTZ: To think, my lord, if you delight not in man, what lenten entertainment the players shall receive from

---

[10] of for on; "I have an eye on you" (Hudson)

you: we coted[11] them on the way; and hither are they

coming, to offer you service.

HAMLET: He that plays the king shall be welcome; his majesty

shall have tribute of me; the adventurous knight

shall use his foil and target; the lover shall not

sigh gratis; the humourous man shall end his part

in peace; the clown shall make those laugh whose

lungs are tickled o' the sere; and the lady shall

say her mind freely, or the blank verse shall halt

for't. What players are they?

ROSENCRANTZ: Even those you were wont to take delight in, the

tragedians of the city.

HAMLET: How chances it they travel? their residence, both

in reputation and profit, was better both ways.

ROSENCRANTZ: I think their inhibition comes by the means of the

late innovation.

HAMLET: Do they hold the same estimation they did when I was

in the city? are they so followed?

ROSENCRANTZ: No, indeed, are they not.

HAMLET: How comes it? do they grow rusty?

ROSENCRANTZ: Nay, their endeavour keeps in the wonted pace: but

there is, sir, an aery of children, little eyases,

that cry out on the top of question, and are most

tyrannically clapped for't: these are now the

fashion, and so berattle the common stages—so they

call them—that many wearing rapiers are afraid of

goose-quills and dare scarce come thither.

---

[11] passed

HAMLET: What, are they children? who maintains 'em? how are

they escoted? Will they pursue the quality no

longer than they can sing? will they not say

afterwards, if they should grow themselves to common

players—as it is most like, if their means are no

better—their writers do them wrong, to make them

exclaim against their own succession?

ROSENCRANTZ: 'Faith, there has been much to do on both sides; and

the nation holds it no sin to tarre them to

controversy: there was, for a while, no money bid

for argument, unless the poet and the player went to

cuffs in the question.

HAMLET: Is't possible?

GUILDENSTERN: O, there has been much throwing about of brains.

HAMLET: Do the boys carry it away?

ROSENCRANTZ: Ay, that they do, my lord; Hercules and his load too.

HAMLET: It is not very strange; for mine uncle is king of

Denmark, and those that would make mows at him while

my father lived, give twenty, forty, fifty, an

hundred ducats a-piece for his picture in little.

'Sblood, there is something in this more than

natural, if philosophy could find it out.

Flourish of trumpets within

GUILDENSTERN: There are the players.

HAMLET: Gentlemen, you are welcome to Elsinore. Your hands,

come then: the appurtenance of welcome is fashion

and ceremony: let me comply with you in this garb,

lest my extent to the players, which, I tell you,

must show fairly outward, should more appear like

entertainment than yours. You are welcome: but my

uncle-father and aunt-mother are deceived.

GUILDENSTERN: In what, my dear lord?

HAMLET: I am but mad north-north-west: when the wind is

southerly I know a hawk from a handsaw.

[Enter POLONIUS]

POLONIUS: Well be with you, gentlemen!

HAMLET: Hark you, Guildenstern; and you too: at each ear a

hearer: that great baby you see there is not yet

out of his swaddling-clouts.

ROSENCRANTZ: Happily he's the second time come to them; for they

say an old man is twice a child.

HAMLET: I will prophesy he comes to tell me of the players;

mark it. You say right, sir: o' Monday morning;

'twas so indeed.

POLONIUS: My lord, I have news to tell you.

HAMLET: My lord, I have news to tell you.

When Roscius was an actor in Rome—

POLONIUS: The actors are come hither, my lord.

HAMLET: Buz, buz!

POLONIUS: Upon mine honour—

HAMLET: Then came each actor on his ass—

POLONIUS: The best actors in the world, either for tragedy,

comedy, history, pastoral, pastoral-comical,

historical-pastoral, tragical-historical, tragical-

comical-historical-pastoral, scene individable, or

poem unlimited: Seneca cannot be too heavy, nor

Plautus too light[12]. For the law of writ and the

liberty, these are the only men.

HAMLET: O Jephthah, judge of Israel, what a treasure hadst thou[13]!

POLONIUS: What a treasure had he, my lord?

HAMLET: Why,

'One fair daughter and no more,

The which he loved passing well.'

POLONIUS: [Aside] Still on my daughter.

HAMLET: Am I not i' the right, old Jephthah?

POLONIUS: If you call me Jephthah, my lord, I have a daughter

that I love passing well.

HAMLET: Nay, that follows not.

POLONIUS: What follows, then, my lord?

HAMLET: Why,

'As by lot, God wot,'

and then, you know,

'It came to pass, as most like it was,'

the first row of the pious chanson will show you

more; for look, where my abridgement comes.

[Enter four or five Players]

You are welcome, masters; welcome, all. I am glad

to see thee well. Welcome, good friends. O, my old

friend! thy face is valenced[14] since I saw thee last:

---

[12] Seneca and Plautus were Roman writers; Seneca wrote tragedies, Plautus comedies (see Hudson)

[13] This and what follows is a lengthy reference to an old ballad called Jeptha, Judge of Israel (Hudson)

[14] Bearded

comest thou to beard me in Denmark? What, my young

lady and mistress! By'r lady, your ladyship is

nearer to heaven than when I saw you last, by the

altitude of a chopine. Pray God, your voice, like

apiece of uncurrent gold, be not cracked within the

ring. Masters, you are all welcome. We'll e'en

to't like French falconers, fly at any thing we see:

we'll have a speech straight: come, give us a taste

of your quality; come, a passionate speech.

FIRST PLAYER: What speech, my lord?

HAMLET: I heard thee speak me a speech once, but it was

never acted; or, if it was, not above once; for the

play, I remember, pleased not the million; 'twas

caviare to the general: but it was—as I received

it, and others, whose judgments in such matters

cried in the top of mine—an excellent play, well

digested in the scenes, set down with as much

modesty as cunning. I remember, one said there

were no sallets in the lines to make the matter

savoury, nor no matter in the phrase that might

indict the author of affectation; but called it an

honest method, as wholesome as sweet, and by very

much more handsome than fine. One speech in it I

chiefly loved: 'twas Aeneas' tale to Dido; and

thereabout of it especially, where he speaks of

Priam's slaughter: if it live in your memory, begin

at this line: let me see, let me see—

'The rugged Pyrrhus, like the Hyrcanian beast,'

it is not so: it begins with Pyrrhus:

'The rugged Pyrrhus, he whose sable arms,

Black as his purpose, did the night resemble

When he lay couched in the ominous horse,

Hath now this dread and black complexion smear'd

With heraldry more dismal; head to foot

Now is he total gules; horridly trick'd

With blood of fathers, mothers, daughters, sons,

Baked and impasted with the parching streets,

That lend a tyrannous and damned light

To their lord's murder: roasted in wrath and fire,

And thus o'er-sized with coagulate gore,

With eyes like carbuncles, the hellish Pyrrhus

Old grandsire Priam seeks.'

So, proceed you.

POLONIUS: 'Fore God, my lord, well spoken, with good accent and good discretion.

FIRST PLAYER: 'Anon he finds him

Striking too short at Greeks; his antique sword,

Rebellious to his arm, lies where it falls,

Repugnant to command: unequal match'd,

Pyrrhus at Priam drives; in rage strikes wide;

But with the whiff and wind of his fell sword

The unnerved father falls. Then senseless Ilium,

Seeming to feel this blow, with flaming top

Stoops to his base, and with a hideous crash

Takes prisoner Pyrrhus' ear: for, lo! his sword,

Which was declining on the milky head

Of reverend Priam, seem'd i' the air to stick:

So, as a painted tyrant, Pyrrhus stood,

And like a neutral to his will and matter,

Did nothing.

But, as we often see, against some storm,

A silence in the heavens, the rack[15] stand still,

The bold winds speechless and the orb below

As hush as death, anon the dreadful thunder

Doth rend the region, so, after Pyrrhus' pause,

Aroused vengeance sets him new a-work;

And never did the Cyclops' hammers fall

On Mars's armour forged for proof eterne[16]

With less remorse than Pyrrhus' bleeding sword

Now falls on Priam.

Out, out, thou strumpet, Fortune! All you gods,

In general synod 'take away her power;

Break all the spokes and fellies from her wheel,

And bowl the round nave down the hill of heaven,

As low as to the fiends!'

POLONIUS: This is too long.

HAMLET: It shall to the barber's, with your beard. Prithee,

say on: he's for a jig[17] or a tale of bawdry, or he

sleeps: say on: come to Hecuba.

FIRST PLAYER: 'But who, O, who had seen the mobled quee—'

HAMLET: 'The mobled queen?'

---

[15] Rack refers to light clouds; all of heaven standing still (Hudson)

[16] Eternal

[17] jester

POLONIUS: That's good; 'mobled queen' is good.

FIRST PLAYER: 'Run barefoot up and down, threatening the flames

With bisson rheum[18]; a clout upon that head

Where late the diadem stood, and for a robe,

About her lank and all o'er-teemed loins,

A blanket, in the alarm of fear caught up;

Who this had seen, with tongue in venom steep'd,

'Gainst Fortune's state would treason have pronounced:

But if the gods themselves did see her then

When she saw Pyrrhus make malicious sport

In mincing with his sword her husband's limbs,

The instant burst of clamour that she made,

Unless things mortal move them not at all,

Would have made milch the burning eyes of heaven,

And passion in the gods.'

POLONIUS: Look, whether he has not turned his colour and has

tears in's eyes. Pray you, no more.

HAMLET: 'Tis well: I'll have thee speak out the rest soon.

Good my lord, will you see the players well

bestowed? Do you hear, let them be well used; for

they are the abstract and brief chronicles of the

time: after your death you were better have a bad

epitaph than their ill report while you live.

POLONIUS: My lord, I will use them according to their desert.

HAMLET: God's bodykins, man, much better: use every man

after his desert, and who should 'scape whipping?

Use them after your own honour and dignity: the less

---

[18] blinding tears (Hudson)

they deserve, the more merit is in your bounty.

Take them in.

POLONIUS: Come, sirs.

HAMLET: Follow him, friends: we'll hear a play to-morrow.

[Exit POLONIUS with all the Players but the First]

Dost thou hear me, old friend; can you play the

Murder of Gonzago?

FIRST PLAYER: Ay, my lord.

HAMLET: We'll ha't to-morrow night. You could, for a need,

study a speech of some dozen or sixteen lines, which

I would set down and insert in't, could you not?

FIRST PLAYER: Ay, my lord.

HAMLET: Very well. Follow that lord; and look you mock him not.

[Exit First Player]

My good friends, I'll leave you till night: you are

welcome to Elsinore.

ROSENCRANTZ: Good my lord!

HAMLET: Ay, so, God be wi' ye;

[Exeunt ROSENCRANTZ and GUILDENSTERN]

Now I am alone.

O, what a rogue and peasant slave am I!

Is it not monstrous that this player here,

But in a fiction, in a dream of passion,

Could force his soul so to his own conceit

That from her working all his visage wann'd,

Tears in his eyes, distraction in's aspect,

A broken voice, and his whole function suiting

With forms to his conceit? and all for nothing!

For Hecuba!

What's Hecuba to him, or he to Hecuba[19],

That he should weep for her? What would he do,

Had he the motive and the cue for passion

That I have? He would drown the stage with tears

And cleave the general ear with horrid speech,

Make mad the guilty and appal the free,

Confound the ignorant, and amaze indeed

The very faculties of eyes and ears. Yet I,

A dull and muddy-mettled rascal, peak,

Like John-a-dreams, unpregnant of my cause,

And can say nothing; no, not for a king,

Upon whose property and most dear life

A damn'd defeat was made. Am I a coward?

Who calls me villain? breaks my pate across?

Plucks off my beard, and blows it in my face?

Tweaks me by the nose? gives me the lie i' the throat,

As deep as to the lungs?[20] who does me this?

Ha!

'Swounds, I should take it: for it cannot be

But I am pigeon-liver'd and lack gall

To make oppression bitter, or ere this

I should have fatted all the region kites

With this slave's offal: bloody, bawdy villain!

Remorseless, treacherous, lecherous, kindless villain!

---

[19] Hamlet is distressed, saying that this actor conjures up more emotion for a fake tragedy than Hamlet can for his real one

[20] This, and much of what follows is a continuation of Hamlet's distressed rant

O, vengeance!

Why, what an ass am I! This is most brave,

That I, the son of a dear father murder'd,

Prompted to my revenge by heaven and hell,

Must, like a whore, unpack my heart with words,

And fall a-cursing, like a very drab,

A scullion!

Fie upon't! foh! About, my brain! I have heard

That guilty creatures sitting at a play

Have by the very cunning of the scene

Been struck so to the soul that presently

They have proclaim'd their malefactions;

For murder, though it have no tongue, will speak

With most miraculous organ. I'll have these players

Play something like the murder of my father

Before mine uncle: I'll observe his looks;

I'll tent him to the quick: if he but blench,

I know my course. The spirit that I have seen

May be the devil: and the devil hath power

To assume a pleasing shape; yea, and perhaps

Out of my weakness and my melancholy,

As he is very potent with such spirits,

Abuses me to damn me: I'll have grounds

More relative than this: the play 's the thing

Wherein I'll catch the conscience of the king.[21]

[Exit]

---

[21] By now Hamlet has devised his master plan to "gain proof" that Claudius killed his father. He hopes it will work.

ACT II ASSESSMENT

Scene 1 often stumps critics. Thematically, not a whole lot is happening. And yet, it exists as one of those unavoidable, yet occasionally awkwardly clumsy and ubiquitous scenes which exist simply for the necessity of laying down plot information. There is a larger political subplot at work in Hamlet that rarely gets much attention (after all, Hamlet is a prince and his father (and subsequent stepfather), Kings—there is some political matter at work after all). These scene serves to service that subplot, and remind us of an external ticking time clock beyond the simpler concerns of our main characters. You'll notice that Shakespeare cleverly tucks this scene right into the slow beginning of a new act.

You'll notice that Scene 2 is notably longer than all other scenes, but also contains some of the most exciting action of the whole play. Shakespeare ends with a likewise cliffhanger flourish, Hamlet finally having thought of a plan by which to gain proof of his uncle's killing of his father. As we move closer and closer to the heart of the play, it becomes easier to observe how each act serves to link the larger story at work for Hamlet.

At the end of Act 1, Hamlet saw his father's ghost and learned that his father was murdered and that his murdered father expects him to avenge his death. In some circles, this is what we would also call an "inciting incident."

Now, at the end of Act 2, Hamlet has reached the point of no return. He is taking a step further onto this journey and is now actively plotting against his uncle.

Dangerous times await…

ACT III SUMMARY

Rosencrantz and Guildenstern check in with the King and Queen, but they are unable to report back anything useful about why Hamlet has been acting strangely. King Claudius and Polonius then decide to try and use Ophelia to get some information out of Hamlet. They hide behind a curtain and eavesdrop on a conversation between the two.

But the moment backfires. Hamlet erupts into an angry tirade toward Ophelia, claiming that he did love her once but that now she's no better than any other woman who can't be trusted (yes, he goes there).

Later, Hamlet invites the King and Queen to watch the play that he has organized with the acting troupe. It is a play about a man murdering a King and then marrying the Queen (Hamlet is making no attempt to be subtle). However, the plot works. Hamlet keeps a firm eye on his uncle during the action of the play, and observes a moment of guilt and fear in his uncle's eyes during the acting of the fictional murder. The scene ends abruptly as Claudius storms out of the room, angered by the insinuations of the play.

Hamlet, however, takes this moment to mean a great victory. He now has proof that his uncle is indeed guilty of murder (since he wasn't quite prepared to accept the word of his father's ghost just yet).

Claudius, meanwhile, takes a moment to think about his own situation. In a monologue in which he thinks he is alone, he confesses outright to having killed his brother and then prays for forgiveness. Hamlet considers killing him now, but then pauses, telling himself that if he kills his uncle in a moment of prayer, his uncle will go to heaven. No, this isn't good enough for Hamlet. He wants to condemn the man to eternal damnation, and he therefore decides to wait and continue to bide his time.

From there, Hamlet goes to meet with his mother Gertrude where he confronts her for having remarried so quickly after the death of her husband. He hears a noise behind a curtain and stabs at it, without realizing that Polonius had been listening behind it. He is horrified by his actions, but then he and his mother continue to argue, before finally reaching a moment of understanding. Hamlet realizes that he will need to go on the run after having accidentally killed an innocent man, but is thankful that he and his mother are finally in agreement about Claudius being a foul person.

ACT III: SCENE I

SCENE I. A room in the castle.

[Enter KING CLAUDIUS, QUEEN GERTRUDE, POLONIUS, OPHELIA, ROSENCRANTZ, and GUILDENSTERN]

KING CLAUDIUS: And can you, by no drift of circumstance,

Get from him why he puts on this confusion,

Grating so harshly all his days of quiet

With turbulent and dangerous lunacy?

ROSENCRANTZ: He does confess he feels himself distracted;

But from what cause he will by no means speak.

GUILDENSTERN: Nor do we find him forward to be sounded,

But, with a crafty madness, keeps aloof,

When we would bring him on to some confession

Of his true state.

QUEEN GERTRUDE: Did he receive you well?

ROSENCRANTZ: Most like a gentleman.

GUILDENSTERN: But with much forcing of his disposition.

ROSENCRANTZ: Niggard of question[1]; but, of our demands,

Most free in his reply.

QUEEN GERTRUDE: Did you assay him?

To any pastime?

ROSENCRANTZ: Madam, it so fell out, that certain players

We o'er-raught[2] on the way: of these we told him;

And there did seem in him a kind of joy

---

[1] ie, did not have questions

[2] Caught up with them

To hear of it: they are about the court,

And, as I think, they have already order

This night to play before him.

POLONIUS: 'Tis most true:

And he beseech'd me to entreat your majesties

To hear and see the matter.

KING CLAUDIUS: With all my heart; and it doth much content me

To hear him so inclined.

Good gentlemen, give him a further edge,

And drive his purpose on to these delights.

ROSENCRANTZ: We shall, my lord.

[Exeunt ROSENCRANTZ and GUILDENSTERN]

KING CLAUDIUS: Sweet Gertrude, leave us too;

For we have closely[3] sent for Hamlet hither,

That he, as 'twere by accident, may here

Affront[4] Ophelia:

Her father and myself, lawful espials,

Will so bestow ourselves that, seeing, unseen,

We may of their encounter frankly judge,

And gather by him, as he is behaved,

If 't be the affliction of his love or no

That thus he suffers for.

QUEEN GERTRUDE: I shall obey you.

And for your part, Ophelia, I do wish

---

3 Secretly

4 Talk to

That your good beauties be the happy cause

Of Hamlet's wildness: so shall I hope your virtues

Will bring him to his wonted way again,

To both your honours.

OPHELIA: Madam, I wish it may.

[Exit QUEEN GERTRUDE]

POLONIUS: Ophelia, walk you here. Gracious, so please you,

We will bestow ourselves. [To OPHELIA] Read on this book;

That show of such an exercise may colour

Your loneliness. We are oft to blame in this,—

'Tis too much proved—that with devotion's visage

And pious action we do sugar o'er

The devil himself.

KING CLAUDIUS: [Aside] O, 'tis too true!

How smart a lash that speech doth give my conscience!

The harlot's cheek, beautied with plastering art,

Is not more ugly to the thing that helps it

Than is my deed to my most painted word:

O heavy burthen!

POLONIUS: I hear him coming: let's withdraw, my lord.

[Exeunt KING CLAUDIUS and POLONIUS

Enter HAMLET]

HAMLET: To be, or not to be, that is the question,

Whether 'tis nobler in the mind to suffer

The slings and arrows of outrageous fortune,

Or to take arms against a sea of troubles,

And by opposing end them? To die: to sleep;

No more; and by a sleep to say we end

The heart-ache and the thousand natural shocks

That flesh is heir to, 'tis a consummation

Devoutly to be wish'd. To die, to sleep;

To sleep: perchance to dream: ay, there's the rub[5];

For in that sleep of death what dreams may come

When we have shuffled off this mortal coil,

Must give us pause: there's the respect

That makes calamity of so long life;

For who would bear the whips and scorns of time,

The oppressor's wrong, the proud man's contumely,

The pangs of despised love, the law's delay,

The insolence of office and the spurns

That patient merit of the unworthy takes,

When he himself might his quietus make

With a bare bodkin[6]? who would fardels[7] bear,

To grunt and sweat under a weary life,

But that the dread of something after death,

The undiscover'd country from whose bourn

No traveller returns, puzzles the will

And makes us rather bear those ills we have

Than fly to others that we know not of?

Thus conscience does make cowards of us all;

---

[5] hindrance (Hudson)

[6] Dagger

[7] Burdens

And thus the native hue of resolution

Is sicklied o'er with the pale cast of thought,

And enterprises of great pith and moment

With this regard their currents turn awry,

And lose the name of action—Soft you now!

The fair Ophelia! Nymph, in thy orisons

Be all my sins remember'd.

OPHELIA: Good my lord,

How does your honour for this many a day?

HAMLET: I humbly thank you; well, well, well.

OPHELIA: My lord, I have remembrances[8] of yours,

That I have longed long to re-deliver;

I pray you, now receive them.

HAMLET: No, not I;

I never gave you aught[9].

OPHELIA: My honour'd lord, you know right well you did;

And, with them, words of so sweet breath composed

As made the things more rich: their perfume lost,

Take these again; for to the noble mind

Rich gifts wax poor when givers prove unkind.

There, my lord.

HAMLET: Ha, ha! are you honest?

OPHELIA: My lord?

HAMLET: Are you fair?

OPHELIA: What means your lordship?

---

[8] Little gifts

[9] Anything

HAMLET: That if you be honest and fair, your honesty should

admit no discourse to your beauty.

OPHELIA: Could beauty, my lord, have better commerce than

with honesty?

HAMLET: Ay, truly; for the power of beauty will sooner

transform honesty from what it is to a bawd than the

force of honesty can translate beauty into his

likeness: this was sometime a paradox, but now the

time gives it proof. I did love you once.

OPHELIA: Indeed, my lord, you made me believe so.

HAMLET: You should not have believed me; for virtue cannot

so inoculate our old stock but we shall relish of

it: I loved you not.

OPHELIA: I was the more deceived.

HAMLET: Get thee to a nunnery: why wouldst thou be a

breeder of sinners? I am myself indifferent honest;

but yet I could accuse me of such things that it

were better my mother had not borne me: I am very

proud, revengeful, ambitious, with more offences at

my beck than I have thoughts to put them in,

imagination to give them shape, or time to act them

in. What should such fellows as I do crawling

between earth and heaven? We are arrant knaves,

all; believe none of us. Go thy ways to a nunnery.

Where's your father?

OPHELIA: At home, my lord.

HAMLET: Let the doors be shut upon him[10], that he may play the

fool no where but in's own house. Farewell.

OPHELIA: O, help him, you sweet heavens!

HAMLET: If thou dost marry, I'll give thee this plague for

thy dowry: be thou as chaste as ice, as pure as

snow, thou shalt not escape calumny. Get thee to a

nunnery, go: farewell. Or, if thou wilt needs

marry, marry a fool; for wise men know well enough

what monsters you make of them. To a nunnery, go,

and quickly too. Farewell.

OPHELIA: O heavenly powers, restore him!

HAMLET: I have heard of your paintings too, well enough; God

has given you one face, and you make yourselves

another: you jig, you amble, and you lisp, and

nick-name God's creatures, and make your wantonness

your ignorance. Go to, I'll no more on't; it hath

made me mad. I say, we will have no more marriages:

those that are married already, all but one, shall

live; the rest shall keep as they are. To a

nunnery, go.

[Exit]

OPHELIA: O, what a noble mind is here o'erthrown!

The courtier's, soldier's, scholar's, eye, tongue, sword;

The expectancy and rose of the fair state,

The glass of fashion and the mould of form,

The observed of all observers, quite, quite down!

---

[10] Many actors have chosen to play this moment as Hamlet figuring out that Ophelia has lied to him and that Polonius is in fact eavesdropping on their meeting. This helps to explain the rapid change in his tone.

And I, of ladies most deject and wretched,

That suck'd the honey of his music vows,

Now see that noble and most sovereign reason,

Like sweet bells jangled, out of tune and harsh;

That unmatch'd form and feature of blown youth

Blasted with ecstasy: O, woe is me,

To have seen what I have seen, see what I see!

[Re-enter KING CLAUDIUS and POLONIUS]

KING CLAUDIUS: Love! his affections do not that way tend;

Nor what he spake, though it lack'd form a little,

Was not like madness. There's something in his soul,

O'er which his melancholy sits on brood;

And I do doubt the hatch and the disclose

Will be some danger: which for to prevent,

I have in quick determination

Thus set it down: he shall with speed to England,

For the demand of our neglected tribute

Haply the seas and countries different

With variable objects shall expel

This something-settled matter in his heart,

Whereon his brains still beating puts him thus

From fashion of himself. What think you on't?

POLONIUS: It shall do well: but yet do I believe

The origin and commencement of his grief

Sprung from neglected love. How now, Ophelia!

You need not tell us what Lord Hamlet said;

We heard it all. My lord, do as you please;

But, if you hold it fit, after the play

Let his queen mother all alone entreat him

To show his grief: let her be round with him;

And I'll be placed, so please you, in the ear

Of all their conference. If she find him not,

To England send him, or confine him where

Your wisdom best shall think.

KING CLAUDIUS: It shall be so:

Madness in great ones must not unwatch'd go.

[Exeunt]

ACT III: SCENE II

SCENE II. A hall in the castle.

[Enter HAMLET and Players]

HAMLET: Speak the speech, I pray you, as I pronounced it to

you, trippingly on the tongue: but if you mouth it,

as many of your players do, I had as lief the

town-crier spoke my lines[1]. Nor do not saw the air

too much with your hand, thus, but use all gently;

for in the very torrent, tempest, and, as I may say,

the whirlwind of passion, you must acquire and beget

a temperance that may give it smoothness. O, it

offends me to the soul to hear a robustious

periwig-pated fellow tear a passion to tatters, to

very rags, to split the ears of the groundlings, who

for the most part are capable of nothing but

inexplicable dumbshows and noise: I would have such

a fellow whipped for o'erdoing Termagant; it

out-herods Herod: pray you, avoid it.

FIRST PLAYER: I warrant your honour.

HAMLET: Be not too tame neither, but let your own discretion

be your tutor: suit the action to the word, the

word to the action; with this special o'erstep not

the modesty of nature: for any thing so overdone is

from the purpose of playing, whose end, both at the

first and now, was and is, to hold, as 'twere, the

---

[1] Perform it right, otherwise I would prefer someone as unskilled as the town crier spoke the lines I wrote

mirror up to nature; to show virtue her own feature,

scorn her own image, and the very age and body of

the time his form and pressure. Now this overdone,

or come tardy off, though it make the unskilful

laugh, cannot but make the judicious grieve; the

censure of the which one must in your allowance

o'erweigh a whole theatre of others. O, there be

players that I have seen play, and heard others

praise, and that highly, not to speak it profanely,

that, neither having the accent of Christians nor

the gait of Christian, pagan, nor man, have so

strutted and bellowed that I have thought some of

nature's journeymen had made men and not made them

well, they imitated humanity so abominably.

FIRST PLAYER: I hope we have reformed that indifferently with us,
sir.

HAMLET: O, reform it altogether. And let those that play

your clowns speak no more than is set down for them;

for there be of them that will themselves laugh, to

set on some quantity of barren spectators to laugh

too; though, in the mean time, some necessary

question of the play be then to be considered:

that's villanous, and shows a most pitiful ambition

in the fool that uses it. Go, make you ready.

[Exeunt Players

Enter POLONIUS, ROSENCRANTZ, and GUILDENSTERN]

How now, my lord! I will the king hear this piece of work?

POLONIUS: And the queen too, and that presently.

HAMLET: Bid the players make haste.

[Exit POLONIUS]

Will you two help to hasten them?

ROSENCRANTZ/GUILDENSTERN: We will, my lord.

[Exeunt ROSENCRANTZ and GUILDENSTERN]

HAMLET: What ho! Horatio!

[Enter HORATIO]

HORATIO: Here, sweet lord, at your service.

HAMLET: Horatio, thou art e'en as just a man

As e'er my conversation coped withal.

HORATIO: O, my dear lord,—

HAMLET: Nay, do not think I flatter;

For what advancement may I hope from thee

That no revenue hast but thy good spirits,

To feed and clothe thee? Why should the poor be flatter'd?

No, let the candied tongue lick absurd pomp,

And crook the pregnant[2] hinges of the knee

Where thrift may follow fawning. Dost thou hear?

Since my dear soul was mistress of her choice

And could of men distinguish, her election

Hath seal'd thee for herself; for thou hast been

As one, in suffering all, that suffers nothing,

A man that fortune's buffets and rewards

Hast ta'en with equal thanks: and blest are those

---

2 Ready

Whose blood and judgment are so well commingled,

That they are not a pipe for fortune's finger

To sound what stop she please. Give me that man

That is not passion's slave, and I will wear him

In my heart's core, ay, in my heart of heart,

As I do thee.—Something too much of this.—

There is a play to-night before the king;

One scene of it comes near the circumstance

Which I have told thee of my father's death:

I prithee, when thou seest that act afoot,

Even with the very comment of thy soul

Observe mine uncle: if his occulted guilt

Do not itself unkennel in one speech,

It is a damned ghost that we have seen,

And my imaginations are as foul

As Vulcan's stithy[3]. Give him heedful note;

For I mine eyes will rivet to his face,

And after we will both our judgments join

In censure of his seeming.

HORATIO: Well, my lord:

If he steal aught the whilst this play is playing,

And 'scape detecting, I will pay the theft.

HAMLET: They are coming to the play; I must be idle:

Get you a place.

[Danish march. A flourish. Enter KING CLAUDIUS, QUEEN GERTRUDE, POLONIUS, OPHELIA, ROSENCRANTZ, GUILDENSTERN, and others]

---

[3] Vulcan's smith; Vulcan was the Roman equivalent of the god of fire, known for his craft in metallurgy and smithing

KING CLAUDIUS: How fares our cousin Hamlet?

HAMLET: Excellent, i' faith; of the chameleon's dish: I eat

the air, promise-crammed: you cannot feed capons so.

KING CLAUDIUS: I have nothing with this answer, Hamlet; these words

are not mine.

HAMLET: No, nor mine now.

[To POLONIUS] My lord, you played once i' the university, you say?

POLONIUS: That did I, my lord; and was accounted a good actor.

HAMLET: What did you enact?

POLONIUS: I did enact Julius Caesar: I was killed i' the

Capitol; Brutus killed me.

HAMLET: It was a brute part of him to kill so capital a calf

there. Be the players ready?

ROSENCRANTZ: Ay, my lord; they stay upon your patience.

QUEEN GERTRUDE: Come hither, my dear Hamlet, sit by me.

HAMLET: No, good mother, here's metal more attractive.

POLONIUS: [To KING CLAUDIUS] O, ho! do you mark that?

HAMLET: Lady, shall I lie in your lap?

OPHELIA: No, my lord.

HAMLET: I mean, my head upon your lap?

OPHELIA: Ay, my lord.

HAMLET: Do you think I meant country matters?[4]

OPHELIA: I think nothing, my lord.

HAMLET: That's a fair thought to lie between maids' legs.

OPHELIA: What is, my lord?

---

[4] Yes, this is a dirty pun, as is much of what follows in Hamlet's teasing of Ophelia

HAMLET: Nothing.

OPHELIA: You are merry, my lord.

HAMLET: Who, I?

OPHELIA: Ay, my lord.

HAMLET: O God, your only jig-maker. What should a man do
but be merry? for, look you, how cheerfully my
mother looks, and my father died within these two hours.

OPHELIA: Nay, 'tis twice two months, my lord.

HAMLET: So long? Nay then, let the devil wear black, for
I'll have a suit of sables[5]. O heavens! die two
months ago, and not forgotten yet? Then there's
hope a great man's memory may outlive his life half
a year: but, by'r lady, he must build churches,
then; or else shall he suffer not thinking on, with
the hobby-horse, whose epitaph is 'For, O, for, O,
the hobby-horse is forgot.'

[Hautboys play. The dumb-show enters]

*Enter a King and a Queen very lovingly; the Queen embracing him, and
he her. She kneels, and makes show of protestation unto him. He takes
her up, and declines his head upon her neck: lays him down upon a
bank of flowers: she, seeing him asleep, leaves him. Anon comes in a
fellow, takes off his crown, kisses it, and pours poison in the King's
ears, and exit. The Queen returns; finds the King dead, and makes
passionate action. The Poisoner, with some two or three Mutes, comes
in again, seeming to lament with her. The dead body is carried away.
The Poisoner wooes the Queen with gifts: she seems loath and
unwilling awhile, but in the end accepts his love*

[Exeunt]

---

[5] Flashy color

OPHELIA: What means this, my lord?

HAMLET: Marry, this is miching mallecho; it means mischief.

OPHELIA: Belike this show imports the argument[6] of the play.

[Enter Prologue]

HAMLET: We shall know by this fellow: the players cannot

keep counsel; they'll tell all.

OPHELIA: Will he tell us what this show meant?

HAMLET: Ay, or any show that you'll show him: be not you

ashamed to show, he'll not shame to tell you what it means.

OPHELIA: You are naught, you are naught[7]: I'll mark the play.

PROLOGUE: For us, and for our tragedy,

Here stooping to your clemency,

We beg your hearing patiently.

[Exit]

HAMLET: Is this a prologue, or the posy of a ring?

OPHELIA: 'Tis brief, my lord.

HAMLET: As woman's love.

[Enter two Players, King and Queen]

PLAYER KING: Full thirty times hath Phoebus' cart gone round

Neptune's salt wash and Tellus' orbed ground,

And thirty dozen moons with borrow'd sheen

About the world have times twelve thirties been,

Since love our hearts and Hymen did our hands

Unite commutual in most sacred bands.

PLAYER QUEEN: So many journeys may the sun and moon

---

[6] summary

[7] naughty

Make us again count o'er ere love be done!

But, woe is me, you are so sick of late,

So far from cheer and from your former state,

That I distrust you. Yet, though I distrust,

Discomfort you, my lord, it nothing must:

For women's fear and love holds quantity;

In neither aught, or in extremity.

Now, what my love is, proof hath made you know;

And as my love is sized, my fear is so:

Where love is great, the littlest doubts are fear;

Where little fears grow great, great love grows there.

PLAYER KING: 'Faith, I must leave thee, love, and shortly too;

My operant powers their functions leave to do:

And thou shalt live in this fair world behind,

Honour'd, beloved; and haply one as kind

For husband shalt thou—

PLAYER QUEEN: O, confound the rest!

Such love must needs be treason in my breast:

In second husband let me be accurst!

None wed the second but who kill'd the first.

HAMLET: [Aside] Wormwood, wormwood[8].

PLAYER QUEEN: The instances that second marriage move

Are base respects of thrift, but none of love:

A second time I kill my husband dead,

When second husband kisses me in bed.

PLAYER KING: I do believe you think what now you speak;

But what we do determine oft we break.

---

[8] "How awful!"

Purpose is but the slave to memory,

Of violent birth, but poor validity;

Which now, like fruit unripe, sticks on the tree;

But fall, unshaken, when they mellow be.

Most necessary 'tis that we forget

To pay ourselves what to ourselves is debt:

What to ourselves in passion we propose,

The passion ending, doth the purpose lose.

The violence of either grief or joy

Their own enactures[9] with themselves destroy:

Where joy most revels, grief doth most lament;

Grief joys, joy grieves, on slender accident.

This world is not for aye, nor 'tis not strange

That even our loves should with our fortunes change;

For 'tis a question left us yet to prove,

Whether love lead fortune, or else fortune love.

The great man down, you mark his favourite flies;

The poor advanced makes friends of enemies.

And hitherto doth love on fortune tend;

For who not needs shall never lack a friend,

And who in want a hollow friend doth try,

Directly seasons him his enemy.

But, orderly to end where I begun,

Our wills and fates do so contrary run

That our devices still are overthrown;

Our thoughts are ours, their ends none of our own:

So think thou wilt no second husband wed;

---

[9] actions

But die thy thoughts when thy first lord is dead.

PLAYER QUEEN: Nor earth to me give food, nor heaven light!

Sport and repose lock from me day and night!

To desperation turn my trust and hope!

An anchor's cheer in prison be my scope!

Each opposite that blanks the face of joy

Meet what I would have well and it destroy!

Both here and hence pursue me lasting strife,

If, once a widow, ever I be wife!

HAMLET: If she should break it now!

PLAYER KING: 'Tis deeply sworn. Sweet, leave me here awhile;

My spirits grow dull, and fain I would beguile

The tedious day with sleep.

[Sleeps]

PLAYER QUEEN: Sleep rock thy brain,

And never come mischance between us twain!

[Exit]

HAMLET: Madam, how like you this play?

QUEEN GERTRUDE: The lady protests too much, methinks.

HAMLET: O, but she'll keep her word.

KING CLAUDIUS: Have you heard the argument? Is there no offence in 't?

HAMLET: No, no, they do but jest, poison in jest; no offence

i' the world.

KING CLAUDIUS: What do you call the play?

HAMLET: The Mouse-trap. Marry, how? Tropically. This play

is the image of a murder done in Vienna: Gonzago is

the duke's name; his wife, Baptista: you shall see

anon; 'tis a knavish piece of work: but what o'

that? your majesty and we that have free souls, it

touches us not: let the galled jade wince, our

withers are unwrung.

[Enter LUCIANUS]

This is one Lucianus, nephew to the king.

OPHELIA: You are as good as a chorus, my lord.

HAMLET: I could interpret between you and your love, if I

could see the puppets dallying.

OPHELIA: You are keen, my lord, you are keen.

HAMLET: It would cost you a groaning to take off my edge.

OPHELIA: Still better, and worse.

HAMLET: So you must take your husbands. Begin, murderer;

pox, leave thy damnable faces, and begin. Come:

'the croaking raven doth bellow for revenge.'

LUCIANUS: Thoughts black, hands apt, drugs fit, and time agreeing;

Confederate season, else no creature seeing;

Thou mixture rank, of midnight weeds collected,

With Hecate's ban thrice blasted, thrice infected,

Thy natural magic and dire property,

On wholesome life usurp immediately.

Pours the poison into the sleeper's ears

HAMLET: He poisons him i' the garden for's estate. His

name's Gonzago: the story is extant, and writ in

choice Italian: you shall see anon how the murderer

gets the love of Gonzago's wife.

OPHELIA: The king rises.

HAMLET: What, frighted with false fire!

QUEEN GERTRUDE: How fares my lord?

POLONIUS: Give o'er the play.

KING CLAUDIUS: Give me some light: away!

ALL: Lights, lights, lights!

[Exeunt all but HAMLET and HORATIO]

HAMLET: Why, let the stricken deer go weep,

The hart ungalled play;

For some must watch, while some must sleep:

So runs the world away.

Would not this, sir, and a forest of feathers— if

the rest of my fortunes turn Turk with me—with two

Provincial roses on my razed shoes, get me a

fellowship in a cry of players, sir?

HORATIO: Half a share.

HAMLET: A whole one, I.

For thou dost know, O Damon[10] dear,

This realm dismantled was

Of Jove himself; and now reigns here

A very, very—pajock.

HORATIO: You might have rhymed[11].

HAMLET: O good Horatio, I'll take the ghost's word for a

thousand pound. Didst perceive?

HORATIO: Very well, my lord.

HAMLET: Upon the talk of the poisoning?

HORATIO: I did very well note him.

---

[10] Reference to Greek historical figures Damon and Pythias - symbols of enduring friendship

[11] This is a joke - it would have been an easy rhyme for Hamlet to match "was" with "ass" (meaning Claudius) (see Hudson)

HAMLET: Ah, ha! Come, some music! come, the recorders![12]

For if the king like not the comedy,

Why then, belike, he likes it not, perdy.

Come, some music!

[Re-enter ROSENCRANTZ and GUILDENSTERN

GUILDENSTERN]

Good my lord, vouchsafe me a word with you.

HAMLET: Sir, a whole history.

GUILDENSTERN: The king, sir,—

HAMLET: Ay, sir, what of him?

GUILDENSTERN: Is in his retirement marvellous distempered.

HAMLET: With drink, sir?

GUILDENSTERN: No, my lord, rather with choler.

HAMLET: Your wisdom should show itself more richer to

signify this to his doctor; for, for me to put him

to his purgation would perhaps plunge him into far

more choler.

GUILDENSTERN: Good my lord, put your discourse into some frame and

start not so wildly from my affair.

HAMLET: I am tame, sir: pronounce.

GUILDENSTERN: The queen, your mother, in most great affliction of

spirit, hath sent me to you.

HAMLET: You are welcome.

GUILDENSTERN: Nay, good my lord, this courtesy is not of the right

breed. If it shall please you to make me a

wholesome answer, I will do your mother's

---

[12] musical flutes

commandment: if not, your pardon and my return

shall be the end of my business.

HAMLET: Sir, I cannot.

GUILDENSTERN: What, my lord?

HAMLET: Make you a wholesome answer; my wit's diseased: but,

sir, such answer as I can make, you shall command;

or, rather, as you say, my mother: therefore no

more, but to the matter: my mother, you say,—

ROSENCRANTZ: Then thus she says; your behavior hath struck her

into amazement and admiration.

HAMLET: O wonderful son, that can so astonish a mother! But

is there no sequel at the heels of this mother's

admiration? Impart.

ROSENCRANTZ: She desires to speak with you in her closet, ere you

go to bed.

HAMLET: We shall obey, were she ten times our mother. Have

you any further trade with us?

ROSENCRANTZ: My lord, you once did love me.

HAMLET: So I do still, by these pickers and stealers.

ROSENCRANTZ: Good my lord, what is your cause of distemper? you

do, surely, bar the door upon your own liberty, if

you deny your griefs to your friend.

HAMLET: Sir, I lack advancement.

ROSENCRANTZ: How can that be, when you have the voice of the king

himself for your succession in Denmark?

HAMLET: Ay, but sir, 'While the grass grows,'—the proverb

is something musty.

[Re-enter Players with recorders]

O, the recorders! let me see one. To withdraw with

you:—why do you go about to recover the wind of me,

as if you would drive me into a toil[13]?

GUILDENSTERN: O, my lord, if my duty be too bold, my love is too

unmannerly.

HAMLET: I do not well understand that. Will you play upon

this pipe?

GUILDENSTERN: My lord, I cannot.

HAMLET: I pray you.

GUILDENSTERN: Believe me, I cannot.

HAMLET: I do beseech you.

GUILDENSTERN: I know no touch of it, my lord.

HAMLET: 'Tis as easy as lying: govern these ventages[14] with

your lingers and thumb, give it breath with your

mouth, and it will discourse most eloquent music.

Look you, these are the stops[15].

GUILDENSTERN: But these cannot I command to any utterance of

harmony; I have not the skill.

HAMLET: Why, look you now, how unworthy a thing you make of

me! You would play upon me; you would seem to know

my stops; you would pluck out the heart of my

mystery; you would sound me from my lowest note to

the top of my compass: and there is much music,

excellent voice, in this little organ; yet cannot

---

[13] a trap

[14] Holes, for the flute

[15] Again, holes

you make it speak. 'Sblood, do you think I am

easier to be played on than a pipe? Call me what

instrument you will, though you can fret me, yet you

cannot play upon me.[16]

God bless you, sir!

POLONIUS: My lord, the queen would speak with you, and

presently.

HAMLET: Do you see yonder cloud that's almost in shape of a camel?

POLONIUS: By the mass, and 'tis like a camel, indeed.

HAMLET: Methinks it is like a weasel.

POLONIUS: It is backed like a weasel.

HAMLET: Or like a whale?

POLONIUS: Very like a whale.

HAMLET: Then I will come to my mother by and by. They fool

me to the top of my bent[17]. I will come by and by.

POLONIUS: I will say so.

HAMLET: By and by is easily said.

[Exit POLONIUS]

Leave me, friends.

[Exeunt all but HAMLET]

Tis now the very witching time of night,

When churchyards yawn and hell itself breathes out

Contagion to this world: now could I drink hot blood,

---

[16] Hamlet rounds out the metaphor - he knows that Rosencranz and Guildenstern are attempting to trick, or "play" him as easily as an instrument

[17] Hamlet is knowingly spouting nonsense, and Polonius is agreeing with it all, and Hamlet finds this annoying.

And do such bitter business as the day

Would quake to look on. Soft! now to my mother.

O heart, lose not thy nature; let not ever

The soul of Nero[18] enter this firm bosom:

Let me be cruel, not unnatural:

I will speak daggers to her, but use none;

My tongue and soul in this be hypocrites;

How in my words soever she be shent,

To give them seals never, my soul, consent!

[Exit]

---

[18] Emperor Nero killed his mother, who just happened to be married to a ruler named Claudius (Hudson)

ACT III: SCENE III

SCENE III. A room in the castle.

[Enter KING CLAUDIUS, ROSENCRANTZ, and GUILDENSTERN]

KING CLAUDIUS: I like him not, nor stands it safe with us

To let his madness range. Therefore prepare you;

I your commission will forthwith dispatch,

And he to England shall along with you:

The terms of our estate may not endure

Hazard so dangerous as doth hourly grow

Out of his lunacies.

GUILDENSTERN: We will ourselves provide:

Most holy and religious fear it is

To keep those many many bodies safe

That live and feed upon your majesty.

ROSENCRANTZ: The single and peculiar life is bound,

With all the strength and armour of the mind,

To keep itself from noyance; but much more

That spirit upon whose weal depend and rest

The lives of many. The cease of majesty

Dies not alone; but, like a gulf, doth draw

What's near it with it: it is a massy wheel,

Fix'd on the summit of the highest mount,

To whose huge spokes ten thousand lesser things

Are mortised and adjoin'd; which, when it falls,

Each small annexment, petty consequence,

Attends the boisterous ruin. Never alone

Did the king sigh, but with a general groan.

KING CLAUDIUS: Arm you, I pray you, to this speedy voyage;

For we will fetters put upon this fear,

Which now goes too free-footed.

ROSENCRANTZ/GUILDENSTERN: We will haste us.

[Exeunt ROSENCRANTZ and GUILDENSTERN

Enter POLONIUS]

POLONIUS: My lord, he's going to his mother's closet:

Behind the arras I'll convey myself,

To hear the process; and warrant she'll tax him home:

And, as you said, and wisely was it said,

'Tis meet that some more audience than a mother,

Since nature makes them partial, should o'erhear

The speech, of vantage. Fare you well, my liege:

I'll call upon you ere you go to bed,

And tell you what I know.

KING CLAUDIUS: Thanks, dear my lord.

[Exit POLONIUS]

O, my offence is rank it smells to heaven;

It hath the primal eldest curse[1] upon't,

A brother's murder. Pray can I not,

Though inclination be as sharp as will:

My stronger guilt defeats my strong intent;

And, like a man to double business bound,

---

[1] The first oldest curse, referring to the murder of Abel by his own brother Cain (see Genesis 4)

I stand in pause where I shall first begin,

And both neglect. What if this cursed hand

Were thicker than itself with brother's blood,

Is there not rain enough in the sweet heavens

To wash it white as snow? Whereto serves mercy

But to confront the visage of offence?

And what's in prayer but this two-fold force,

To be forestalled ere we come to fall,

Or pardon'd being down? Then I'll look up;

My fault is past. But, O, what form of prayer

Can serve my turn? 'Forgive me my foul murder'?

That cannot be; since I am still possess'd

Of those effects for which I did the murder,

My crown, mine own ambition and my queen.

May one be pardon'd and retain the offence?

In the corrupted currents of this world

Offence's gilded hand may shove by justice,

And oft 'tis seen the wicked prize itself

Buys out the law: but 'tis not so above;

There is no shuffling, there the action lies

In his true nature; and we ourselves compell'd,

Even to the teeth and forehead of our faults,

To give in evidence. What then? what rests?

Try what repentance can: what can it not?

Yet what can it when one can not repent?

O wretched state! O bosom black as death!

O limed soul, that, struggling to be free,

Art more engaged! Help, angels! Make assay!

Bow, stubborn knees; and, heart with strings of steel,

Be soft as sinews of the newborn babe!

All may be well.

[Retires and kneels]

[Enter HAMLET]

HAMLET: Now might I do it pat, now he is praying;

And now I'll do't. And so he goes to heaven;

And so am I revenged. That would be scann'd:[2]

A villain kills my father; and for that,

I, his sole son, do this same villain send

To heaven.

O, this is hire and salary, not revenge.

He took my father grossly, full of bread;

With all his crimes broad blown, as flush as May;

And how his audit stands who knows save heaven?

But in our circumstance and course of thought,

'Tis heavy with him: and am I then revenged,

To take him in the purging of his soul,

When he is fit and season'd for his passage?

No!

Up, sword; and know thou a more horrid hent[3]:

When he is drunk asleep, or in his rage,

Or in the incestuous pleasure of his bed;

At gaming, swearing, or about some act

That has no relish of salvation in't;

---

[2] Interpreted

[3] purpose

Then trip him, that his heels may kick at heaven,

And that his soul may be as damn'd and black

As hell, whereto it goes. My mother stays:

This physic but prolongs thy sickly days.

[Exit]

KING CLAUDIUS: [Rising] My words fly up, my thoughts remain below:

Words without thoughts never to heaven go.

[Exit]

ACT III: SCENE IV

SCENE IV. Queen Gertrude's chambers.

[Enter QUEEN GERTRUDE and POLONIUS]

POLONIUS: He will come straight. Look you lay home to him:

Tell him his pranks have been too broad to bear with,

And that your grace hath screen'd and stood between

Much heat and him. I'll sconce me even here.

Pray you, be round with him.

HAMLET: [Within] Mother, mother, mother!

QUEEN GERTRUDE: I'll warrant you,

Fear me not: withdraw, I hear him coming.

[POLONIUS hides behind the arras

Enter HAMLET]

HAMLET: Now, mother, what's the matter?

QUEEN GERTRUDE: Hamlet, thou hast thy father much offended.

HAMLET: Mother, you have my father much offended.

QUEEN GERTRUDE: Come, come, you answer with an idle tongue.

HAMLET: Go, go, you question with a wicked tongue.

QUEEN GERTRUDE: Why, how now, Hamlet!

HAMLET: What's the matter now?

QUEEN GERTRUDE: Have you forgot me?

HAMLET: No, by the rood, not so:

You are the queen, your husband's brother's wife;

And—would it were not so!—you are my mother.

QUEEN GERTRUDE: Nay, then, I'll set those to you that can speak.

HAMLET: Come, come, and sit you down; you shall not budge;

You go not till I set you up a glass

Where you may see the inmost part of you.

QUEEN GERTRUDE: What wilt thou do? thou wilt not murder me?

Help, help, ho!

POLONIUS: [Behind] What, ho! help, help, help!

HAMLET: [Drawing] How now! a rat? Dead, for a ducat, dead!

Makes a pass through the arras

POLONIUS: [Behind] O, I am slain!

[Falls and dies]

QUEEN GERTRUDE: O me, what hast thou done?

HAMLET: Nay, I know not:

Is it the king?

QUEEN GERTRUDE: O, what a rash and bloody deed is this!

HAMLET: A bloody deed! almost as bad, good mother,

As kill a king, and marry with his brother.

QUEEN GERTRUDE: As kill a king!

HAMLET: Ay, lady, 'twas my word.

[Lifts up the array and discovers POLONIUS]

Thou wretched, rash, intruding fool, farewell!

I took thee for thy better: take thy fortune;

Thou find'st to be too busy is some danger.

Leave wringing of your hands: peace! sit you down,

And let me wring your heart; for so I shall,

If it be made of penetrable stuff,

If damned custom have not brass'd it so

That it is proof and bulwark against sense.

QUEEN GERTRUDE: What have I done, that thou darest wag thy tongue

In noise so rude against me?

HAMLET: Such an act

That blurs the grace and blush of modesty,

Calls virtue hypocrite, takes off the rose

From the fair forehead of an innocent love

And sets a blister there, makes marriage-vows

As false as dicers' oaths: O, such a deed

As from the body of contraction plucks

The very soul, and sweet religion makes

A rhapsody of words: heaven's face doth glow:

Yea, this solidity and compound mass,

With tristful visage, as against the doom,

Is thought-sick at the act.

QUEEN GERTRUDE: Ay me, what act,

That roars so loud, and thunders in the index?

HAMLET: Look here, upon this picture, and on this,

The counterfeit presentment of two brothers.

See, what a grace was seated on this brow;

Hyperion's curls; the front of Jove himself;

An eye like Mars, to threaten and command;

A station like the herald Mercury

New-lighted on a heaven-kissing hill;

A combination and a form indeed,

Where every god did seem to set his seal,

To give the world assurance of a man:

This was your husband. Look you now, what follows:

Here is your husband; like a mildew'd ear,

Blasting his wholesome brother. Have you eyes?

Could you on this fair mountain leave to feed,

And batten on this moor? Ha! have you eyes?

You cannot call it love; for at your age

The hey-day in the blood is tame, it's humble,

And waits upon the judgment: and what judgment

Would step from this to this? Sense, sure, you have,

Else could you not have motion; but sure, that sense

Is apoplex'd; for madness would not err,

Nor sense to ecstasy was ne'er so thrall'd

But it reserved some quantity of choice,

To serve in such a difference. What devil was't

That thus hath cozen'd you at hoodman-blind?[1]

Eyes without feeling, feeling without sight,

Ears without hands or eyes, smelling sans all,

Or but a sickly part of one true sense

Could not so mope.

O shame! where is thy blush? Rebellious hell,

If thou canst mutine in a matron's bones,

To flaming youth let virtue be as wax,

And melt in her own fire: proclaim no shame

When the compulsive ardour gives the charge,

Since frost itself as actively doth burn

And reason panders will.

QUEEN GERTRUDE: O Hamlet, speak no more:

---

[1] Much of this rant is Hamlet questioning his mother about how she could have ever thought
Claudius was a worthy husband

Thou turn'st mine eyes into my very soul;

And there I see such black and grained spots

As will not leave their tinct.

HAMLET: Nay, but to live

In the rank sweat of an enseamed bed,

Stew'd in corruption, honeying and making love

Over the nasty sty—

QUEEN GERTRUDE: O, speak to me no more;

These words, like daggers, enter in mine ears;

No more, sweet Hamlet!

HAMLET: A murderer and a villain;

A slave that is not twentieth part the tithe

Of your precedent lord; a vice of kings;

A cutpurse of the empire and the rule,

That from a shelf the precious diadem stole,

And put it in his pocket!

QUEEN GERTRUDE: No more!

HAMLET: A king of shreds and patches—

[Enter Ghost]

Save me, and hover o'er me with your wings,

You heavenly guards! What would your gracious figure?

QUEEN GERTRUDE: Alas, he's mad!

HAMLET: Do you not come your tardy son to chide,

That, lapsed in time and passion, lets go by

The important acting of your dread command? O, say!

GHOST: Do not forget: this visitation

Is but to whet thy almost blunted purpose.

But, look, amazement on thy mother sits:

O, step between her and her fighting soul:

Conceit in weakest bodies strongest works:

Speak to her, Hamlet.

HAMLET: How is it with you, lady?

QUEEN GERTRUDE: Alas, how is't with you,

That you do bend your eye on vacancy

And with the incorporal air do hold discourse?[2]

Forth at your eyes your spirits wildly peep;

And, as the sleeping soldiers in the alarm,

Your bedded hair, like life in excrements,

Starts up, and stands on end. O gentle son,

Upon the heat and flame of thy distemper

Sprinkle cool patience. Whereon do you look?

HAMLET: On him, on him! Look you, how pale he glares!

His form and cause conjoin'd, preaching to stones,

Would make them capable. Do not look upon me;

Lest with this piteous action you convert

My stern effects: then what I have to do

Will want true colour; tears perchance for blood.

QUEEN GERTRUDE: To whom do you speak this?

HAMLET: Do you see nothing there?

QUEEN GERTRUDE: Nothing at all; yet all that is I see.

HAMLET: Nor did you nothing hear?

QUEEN GERTRUDE: No, nothing but ourselves.

HAMLET: Why, look you there! look, how it steals away!

My father, in his habit as he lived!

---

[2] The typical interpretation is that only Hamlet is aware of this appearance of the ghost. Gertrude sees nothing and things her son is talking to the "incorporeal" — bodiless — air

Look, where he goes, even now, out at the portal!

[Exit Ghost]

QUEEN GERTRUDE: This the very coinage[3] of your brain:

This bodiless creation ecstasy

Is very cunning in.

HAMLET: Ecstasy!

My pulse, as yours, doth temperately keep time,

And makes as healthful music: it is not madness

That I have utter'd: bring me to the test,

And I the matter will re-word; which madness

Would gambol from. Mother, for love of grace,

Lay not that mattering unction to your soul,

That not your trespass, but my madness speaks:

It will but skin and film the ulcerous place,

Whilst rank corruption, mining all within,

Infects unseen. Confess yourself to heaven;

Repent what's past; avoid what is to come;

And do not spread the compost on the weeds,

To make them ranker. Forgive me this my virtue;

For in the fatness of these pursy times

Virtue itself of vice must pardon beg,

Yea, curb and woo for leave to do him good.

QUEEN GERTRUDE: O Hamlet, thou hast cleft my heart in twain.

HAMLET: O, throw away the worser part of it,

And live the purer with the other half.

Good night: but go not to mine uncle's bed;

Assume a virtue, if you have it not.

---

[3] Creation

That monster, custom, who all sense doth eat,

Of habits devil, is angel yet in this,

That to the use of actions fair and good

He likewise gives a frock or livery,

That aptly is put on. Refrain to-night,

And that shall lend a kind of easiness

To the next abstinence: the next more easy;

For use almost can change the stamp of nature,

And either shame the devil, or throw him out

With wondrous potency. Once more, good night:

And when you are desirous to be bless'd,

I'll blessing beg of you. For this same lord,

[Pointing to POLONIUS]

I do repent: but heaven hath pleased it so,

To punish me with this and this with me,

That I must be their scourge and minister.

I will bestow him, and will answer well

The death I gave him. So, again, good night.

I must be cruel, only to be kind:

Thus bad begins and worse remains behind.

One word more, good lady.

QUEEN GERTRUDE: What shall I do?

HAMLET: Not this, by no means, that I bid you do:

Let the bloat king tempt you again to bed;

Pinch wanton on your cheek; call you his mouse;

And let him, for a pair of reechy kisses,

Or paddling in your neck with his damn'd fingers,

Make you to ravel all this matter out,

That I essentially am not in madness,

But mad in craft. 'Twere good you let him know;

For who, that's but a queen, fair, sober, wise,

Would from a paddock, from a bat, a gib,

Such dear concernings hide? who would do so?

No, in despite of sense and secrecy,

Unpeg the basket on the house's top.

Let the birds fly, and, like the famous ape,

To try conclusions, in the basket creep,

And break your own neck down.

QUEEN GERTRUDE: Be thou assured, if words be made of breath,

And breath of life, I have no life to breathe

What thou hast said to me.

HAMLET: I must to England[4]; you know that?

QUEEN GERTRUDE: Alack,

I had forgot: 'tis so concluded on.

HAMLET: There's letters seal'd: and my two schoolfellows,

Whom I will trust as I will adders fang'd,

They bear the mandate; they must sweep my way,

And marshal me to knavery. Let it work;

For 'tis the sport to have the engineer

Hoist with his own petard: and 't shall go hard

But I will delve one yard below their mines,

And blow them at the moon: O, 'tis most sweet,

When in one line two crafts directly meet.

This man shall set me packing:

I'll lug the guts into the neighbor room.

---

4 The verb is ellipsed — "I must *go* to England"

Mother, good night. Indeed this counsellor

Is now most still, most secret and most grave,

Who was in life a foolish prating knave.

Come, sir, to draw toward an end with you.

Good night, mother.

[Exeunt; HAMLET dragging in POLONIUS]

ACT III ASSESSMENT

Whew! The action is heating up. In terms of the progression of his revenge, Hamlet has finally obtained the proof needed to believe that his uncle is guilty of murder. He almost killed him but then came up with a reason why the timing wasn't right just yet.

Welcome to what critics have dubbed "the delay" - a tricky part of the play where Hamlet fakes madness, is a jerk to those who love him, broods poetically in dark corners and engages in all around shenanigans before getting down to business (in the thematic parallel of *The Lion King*, you could think of this as Hamlet's Hakuna Matata time).

Writers typically avoid moments like these, as they feel that they can drag on with no advancement of plot. Fortunately, Hamlet knows how to fill his with puns and artful soliloquies and all around silliness which helps the time pass.

This act contains other monumental scenes such as the "Get thee to a nunnery!" scene with Ophelia, as well as the acting of the play within a play. Likewise, Hamlet's confrontation of his mother and subsequent stabbing of Polonius is also a scene known for high drama and tense emotion.

A point of discussion concerning Act III is whether or not Hamlet's "antic disposition" may or may not be finally taking over. Is he still pretending to be mad or is he actually mad? Scholars have made arguments for both sides over the past several hundred years. What do you think?

(See T.S. Eliot's famous essay "Hamlet and His Problems" for a discussion on the thematic issues with presenting a character who pretends to be mad without having any way of gauging whether or not his madness is feigned or real).

Notes for later discussion: This "delay" is actually a somewhat controversial topic of discussion within criticism circles involving the discussion of *Hamlet*. Why does it exist in the first place? According to Aristotelian principles of form and narratology, it has no purpose and therefore should not exist.

But of course, some critics have sought to look beneath the surface of the text and expound upon why this moment exists in the first place. What is your theory? There is no wrong answer, because no one has discovered the right one yet!

ACT IV SUMMARY

Much of the beginning of Act IV is a series of cat-and-mouse scenes—Gertrude conveys the news that Hamlet has killed Polonius. Claudius and others attempt to find out where Hamlet hid Polonius's body (to which Hamlet makes a series of off-color jokes, only furthering both his dark humor as well as his "antic disposition"). Finally, both Hamlet and the body are found, and Claudius sends Hamlet away to England to keep him out of sight.

The political element of the play intervenes for a moment as we reconnect with Fortinbras and his military adventures. Back in Denmark, we learn that Ophelia has sunk to true madness upon learning that her once beloved Hamlet has killed her father Polonius. She wanders around the castle, singing songs and handing out flowers, and doesn't seem to know where she is.

Soon, Laertes returns, furious at having learned of his father's death. At first he blames Claudius who cleverly shifts the blame onto Hamlet where it belongs. A message soon arrives to tell Claudius that Hamlet has escaped from the guards who were escorting him to England, and that he is on his way back home to Denmark.

Claudius, now fully aware that his nephew means him harm, decides to use Laertes' anger to his own advantage. He devises a plot of his own whereby Laertes can avenge his own father's death by killing Hamlet. He suggests that Laertes engage Hamlet in a fencing match, and that Laertes stab his opponent with a poisoned foil. If the poisoned foil doesn't work, Claudius also suggests poisoning Hamlet directly with tainted wine. Laertes agrees. The Act ends with Queen Gertrude breaking in to tell us that Ophelia has drowned herself.

ACT IV: SCENE I

SCENE I. A room in the castle.

[Enter KING CLAUDIUS, QUEEN GERTRUDE, ROSENCRANTZ, and GUILDENSTERN]

KING CLAUDIUS: There's matter in these sighs, these profound heaves:

You must translate: 'tis fit we understand them.

Where is your son?

QUEEN GERTRUDE: Bestow this place on us a little while.

[Exeunt ROSENCRANTZ and GUILDENSTERN]

Ah, my good lord, what have I seen to-night!

KING CLAUDIUS: What, Gertrude? How does Hamlet?

QUEEN GERTRUDE: Mad as the sea and wind, when both contend

Which is the mightier: in his lawless fit,

Behind the arras hearing something stir,

Whips out his rapier, cries, 'A rat, a rat!'

And, in this brainish[1] apprehension, kills

The unseen good old man.

KING CLAUDIUS: O heavy deed!

It had been so with us, had we been there:

His liberty is full of threats to all;

To you yourself, to us, to every one.

Alas, how shall this bloody deed be answer'd?

It will be laid to us, whose providence

Should have kept short, restrain'd and out of haunt[2],

---

[1] Brainsick; crazy (Hudson)

[2] out of the way

This mad young man: but so much was our love,

We would not understand what was most fit;

But, like the owner of a foul disease,

To keep it from divulging, let it feed

Even on the pith of Life. Where is he gone?

QUEEN GERTRUDE: To draw apart the body he hath kill'd:

O'er whom his very madness, like some ore

Among a mineral of metals base,

Shows itself pure; he weeps for what is done.

KING CLAUDIUS: O Gertrude, come away!

The sun no sooner shall the mountains touch,

But we will ship him hence: and this vile deed

We must, with all our majesty and skill,

Both countenance and excuse. Ho, Guildenstern!

[Re-enter ROSENCRANTZ and GUILDENSTERN]

Friends both, go join you with some further aid:

Hamlet in madness hath Polonius slain,

And from his mother's closet hath he dragg'd him:

Go seek him out; speak fair, and bring the body

Into the chapel. I pray you, haste in this.

[Exeunt ROSENCRANTZ and GUILDENSTERN]

Come, Gertrude, we'll call up our wisest friends;

And let them know, both what we mean to do,

And what's untimely done. O, come away!

My soul is full of discord and dismay.

[Exeunt]

ACT IV: SCENE II

SCENE II. Elsinore Castle - A room.

[Enter HAMLET]

HAMLET: Safely stowed.

ROSENCRANTZ/GUILDENSTERN: [Within] Hamlet! Lord Hamlet!

HAMLET: What noise? who calls on Hamlet?

O, here they come.

[Enter ROSENCRANTZ and GUILDENSTERN]

ROSENCRANTZ: What have you done, my lord, with the dead body?

HAMLET: Compounded it with dust, whereto 'tis kin.

ROSENCRANTZ: Tell us where 'tis, that we may take it thence

And bear it to the chapel.

HAMLET: Do not believe it.

ROSENCRANTZ: Believe what?

HAMLET: That I can keep your counsel and not mine own.

Besides, to be demanded of a sponge! what

replication should be made by the son of a king?

ROSENCRANTZ: Take you me for a sponge, my lord?

HAMLET: Ay, sir, that soaks up the king's countenance, his

rewards, his authorities. But such officers do the

king best service in the end: he keeps them, like

an ape, in the corner of his jaw; first mouthed, to

be last swallowed: when he needs what you have

gleaned, it is but squeezing you, and, sponge, you

shall be dry again.

ROSENCRANTZ: I understand you not, my lord.

HAMLET: I am glad of it: a knavish speech sleeps in a

foolish ear.

ROSENCRANTZ: My lord, you must tell us where the body is, and go

with us to the king.

HAMLET: The body is with the king, but the king is not with

the body. The king is a thing—

GUILDENSTERN: A thing, my lord!

HAMLET: Of nothing: bring me to him. Hide fox, and all after.[1]

[Exeunt]

---

[1] Old name for "hide and seek;" Hamlet is continuing to be flippant about having killed Polonius

ACT IV: SCENE III

SCENE III. Another room in the castle.

[Enter KING CLAUDIUS, attended]

KING CLAUDIUS: I have sent to seek him, and to find the body.

How dangerous is it that this man goes loose!

Yet must not we put the strong law on him:

He's loved of the distracted multitude,

Who like not in their judgment, but their eyes;

And where tis so, the offender's scourge is weigh'd,

But never the offence. To bear all smooth and even,

This sudden sending him away must seem

Deliberate pause: diseases desperate grown

By desperate appliance are relieved,

Or not at all.

[Enter ROSENCRANTZ]

How now! what hath befall'n?

ROSENCRANTZ: Where the dead body is bestow'd, my lord,

We cannot get from him.

KING CLAUDIUS: But where is he?

ROSENCRANTZ: Without, my lord; guarded, to know your pleasure.

KING CLAUDIUS: Bring him before us.

ROSENCRANTZ: Ho, Guildenstern! bring in my lord.

[Enter HAMLET and GUILDENSTERN]

KING CLAUDIUS: Now, Hamlet, where's Polonius?

HAMLET: At supper.

KING CLAUDIUS: At supper! where?

HAMLET: Not where he eats, but where he is eaten: a certain convocation of politic worms are e'en at him. Your

worm is your only emperor for diet: we fat all

creatures else to fat us, and we fat ourselves for

maggots: your fat king and your lean beggar is but

variable service, two dishes, but to one table:

that's the end.

KING CLAUDIUS: Alas, alas!

HAMLET: A man may fish with the worm that hath eat of a

king, and eat of the fish that hath fed of that worm.

KING CLAUDIUS: What dost you mean by this?

HAMLET: Nothing but to show you how a king may go a

progress through the guts of a beggar.

KING CLAUDIUS: Where is Polonius?

HAMLET: In heaven; send hither to see: if your messenger

find him not there, seek him i' the other place

yourself. But indeed, if you find him not within

this month, you shall nose him as you go up the

stairs into the lobby.

KING CLAUDIUS: [To Attendants] Go seek him there.

HAMLET: He will stay till ye come.

[Exeunt Attendants]

KING CLAUDIUS: Hamlet, this deed, for thine especial safety—

Which we do tender, as we dearly grieve

For that which thou hast done—must send thee hence

With fiery quickness: therefore prepare thyself;

The bark is ready, and the wind at help,

The associates tend, and every thing is bent

For England.

HAMLET: For England!

KING CLAUDIUS: Ay, Hamlet.

HAMLET: Good.

KING CLAUDIUS: So is it, if thou knew'st our purposes.

HAMLET: I see a cherub that sees them. But, come; for

England! Farewell, dear mother.

KING CLAUDIUS: Thy loving father, Hamlet.

HAMLET: My mother: father and mother is man and wife; man

and wife is one flesh; and so, my mother. Come, for England!

[Exit]

KING CLAUDIUS: Follow him at foot; tempt him with speed aboard;

Delay it not; I'll have him hence to-night:

Away! for every thing is seal'd and done

That else leans on the affair: pray you, make haste.

[Exeunt ROSENCRANTZ and GUILDENSTERN]

And, England, if my love thou hold'st at aught—

As my great power thereof may give thee sense,

Since yet thy cicatrice looks raw and red

After the Danish sword, and thy free awe

Pays homage to us—thou mayst not coldly set

Our sovereign process; which imports at full,

By letters congruing to that effect,

The present death of Hamlet. Do it, England;

For like the hectic in my blood he rages,

And thou must cure me: till I know 'tis done,

Howe'er my haps, my joys were ne'er begun.

[Exit]

ACT IV: SCENE IV

SCENE IV. A plain in Denmark.

[Enter FORTINBRAS, a Captain, and Soldiers, marching]

FORTINBRAS: Go, captain, from me greet the Danish king;

　　Tell him that, by his licence, Fortinbras

　　Craves the conveyance of a promised march

　　Over his kingdom. You know the rendezvous.

　　If that his majesty would aught with us,

　　We shall express our duty in his eye;

　　And let him know so.

CAPTAIN: I will do't, my lord.

FORTINBRAS: Go softly on.

[Exeunt FORTINBRAS and Soldiers

Enter HAMLET, ROSENCRANTZ, GUILDENSTERN, and others]

HAMLET: Good sir, whose powers are these?

CAPTAIN: They are of Norway, sir.

HAMLET: How purposed, sir, I pray you?

CAPTAIN: Against some part of Poland.

HAMLET: Who commands them, sir?

CAPTAIN: The nephews to old Norway, Fortinbras.

HAMLET: Goes it against the main of Poland, sir,

　　Or for some frontier?

CAPTAIN: Truly to speak, and with no addition,

　　We go to gain a little patch of ground

　　That hath in it no profit but the name.

To pay five ducats, five, I would not farm it;

Nor will it yield to Norway or the Pole

A ranker rate, should it be sold in fee.

HAMLET: Why, then the Polack never will defend it.

CAPTAIN: Yes, it is already garrison'd.

HAMLET: Two thousand souls and twenty thousand ducats

Will not debate the question of this straw:

This is the imposthume of much wealth and peace,

That inward breaks, and shows no cause without

Why the man dies. I humbly thank you, sir.

CAPTAIN: God be wi' you, sir.

[Exit]

ROSENCRANTZ: Wilt please you go, my lord?

HAMLET: I'll be with you straight go a little before.

[Exeunt all except HAMLET]

How all occasions do inform against me,

And spur my dull revenge! What is a man,

If his chief good and market of his time

Be but to sleep and feed? a beast, no more.

Sure, he that made us with such large discourse,

Looking before and after, gave us not

That capability and god-like reason

To fust in us unused. Now, whether it be

Bestial oblivion, or some craven scruple

Of thinking too precisely on the event,

A thought which, quarter'd, hath but one part wisdom

And ever three parts coward, I do not know

Why yet I live to say 'This thing's to do;'

Sith I have cause and will and strength and means

To do't. Examples gross as earth exhort me:

Witness this army of such mass and charge

Led by a delicate and tender prince,

Whose spirit with divine ambition puff'd

Makes mouths at the invisible event,

Exposing what is mortal and unsure

To all that fortune, death and danger dare,

Even for an egg-shell. Rightly to be great

Is not to stir without great argument,

But greatly to find quarrel in a straw

When honour's at the stake. How stand I then,

That have a father kill'd, a mother stain'd,

Excitements of my reason and my blood,

And let all sleep? while, to my shame, I see

The imminent death of twenty thousand men,

That, for a fantasy and trick of fame,

Go to their graves like beds, fight for a plot

Whereon the numbers cannot try the cause,

Which is not tomb enough and continent

To hide the slain? O, from this time forth,

My thoughts be bloody, or be nothing worth!

[Exit]

ACT IV: SCENE V

SCENE V. Elsinore. A room in the castle.

[Enter QUEEN GERTRUDE, HORATIO, and a GENTLEMAN]

QUEEN GERTRUDE: I will not speak with her.

GENTLEMAN: She is importunate, indeed distract[1]:

Her mood will needs be pitied.

QUEEN GERTRUDE: What would she have?

GENTLEMAN: She speaks much of her father; says she hears

There's tricks i' the world; and hems, and beats her heart;

Spurns enviously at straws; speaks things in doubt,

That carry but half sense: her speech is nothing,

Yet the unshaped use of it doth move

The hearers to collection; they aim at it,

And botch the words up fit to their own thoughts;

Which, as her winks, and nods, and gestures

yield them,

Indeed would make one think there might be thought,

Though nothing sure, yet much unhappily.

HORATIO: 'Twere good she were spoken with; for she may strew

Dangerous conjectures in ill-breeding minds.

QUEEN GERTRUDE: Let her come in.

[Exit HORATIO]

To my sick soul, as sin's true nature is,

Each toy seems prologue to some great amiss:

---

[1] distracted

So full of artless jealousy is guilt,

It spills itself in fearing to be spilt.

[Re-enter HORATIO, with OPHELIA]

OPHELIA: Where is the beauteous majesty of Denmark?

QUEEN GERTRUDE: How now, Ophelia!

OPHELIA: [Sings]   How should I your true love know

From another one?

By his cockle hat and staff,

And his sandal shoon.

QUEEN GERTRUDE: Alas, sweet lady, what imports this song?

OPHELIA: Say you? nay, pray you, mark.   [Sings]

He is dead and gone, lady,

He is dead and gone;

At his head a grass-green turf,

At his heels a stone.

QUEEN GERTRUDE: Nay, but, Ophelia—

OPHELIA: Pray you, mark.

[Sings] White his shroud as the mountain snow—

[Enter KING CLAUDIUS]

QUEEN GERTRUDE: Alas, look here, my lord.

OPHELIA: [Sings]   Larded[2] with sweet flowers

Which bewept to the grave did go

With true-love showers.

---

[2] Decorated

KING CLAUDIUS: How do you, pretty lady?

OPHELIA: Well, God 'ild you! They say the owl was a baker's

daughter. Lord, we know what we are, but know not

what we may be. God be at your table!

KING CLAUDIUS: Conceit upon her father.

OPHELIA: Pray you, let's have no words of this; but when they

ask you what it means, say you this:

[Sings]   To-morrow is Saint Valentine's day,

All in the morning betime,

And I a maid at your window,

To be your Valentine.

Then up he rose, and donn'd his clothes,

And dupp'd the chamber-door;

Let in the maid, that out a maid

Never departed more.

KING CLAUDIUS: Pretty Ophelia!

OPHELIA: Indeed, la, without an oath, I'll make an end on't:

[Sings]   By Gis and by Saint Charity,

Alack, and fie for shame!

Young men will do't, if they come to't;

By cock, they are to blame.

Quoth she, before you tumbled me,

You promised me to wed.

So would I ha' done, by yonder sun,

An thou hadst not come to my bed.

KING CLAUDIUS: How long hath she been thus?

OPHELIA: I hope all will be well. We must be patient: but I

cannot choose but weep, to think they should lay him

i' the cold ground. My brother shall know of it:

and so I thank you for your good counsel. Come, my

coach! Good night, ladies; good night, sweet ladies;

good night, good night.

[Exit]

KING CLAUDIUS: Follow her close; give her good watch,

I pray you.

[Exit HORATIO]

O, this is the poison of deep grief; it springs

All from her father's death. O Gertrude, Gertrude,

When sorrows come, they come not single spies

But in battalions. First, her father slain:

Next, your son gone; and he most violent author

Of his own just remove: the people muddied,

Thick and unwholesome in their thoughts and whispers,

For good Polonius' death; and we have done but greenly,

In hugger-mugger to inter him: poor Ophelia

Divided from herself and her fair judgment,

Without the which we are pictures, or mere beasts:

Last, and as much containing as all these,

Her brother is in secret come from France;

Feeds on his wonder, keeps himself in clouds,

And wants not buzzers to infect his ear

With pestilent speeches of his father's death;

Wherein necessity, of matter beggar'd,

Will nothing stick our person to arraign

In ear and ear. O my dear Gertrude, this,

Like to a murdering-piece, in many places

Gives me superfluous death.

[A noise within]

QUEEN GERTRUDE: Alack, what noise is this?

KING CLAUDIUS: Where are my Switzers[3]? Let them guard the door.

[Enter another Gentleman]

What is the matter?

GENTLEMAN: Save yourself, my lord:

The ocean, overpeering of his list,

Eats not the flats with more impetuous haste

Than young Laertes, in a riotous head,

O'erbears your officers. The rabble call him lord;

And, as the world were now but to begin,

Antiquity forgot, custom not known,

The ratifiers and props of every word,

They cry 'Choose we: Laertes shall be king:'

Caps, hands, and tongues, applaud it to the clouds:

'Laertes shall be king, Laertes king!'

QUEEN GERTRUDE: How cheerfully on the false trail they cry!

O, this is counter, you false Danish dogs!

KING CLAUDIUS: The doors are broke.

[Noise within]

[Enter LAERTES, armed; Danes following]

LAERTES: Where is this king? Sirs, stand you all without.

DANES: No, let's come in.

---

[3] guards

LAERTES: I pray you, give me leave.

DANES: We will, we will.

They retire without the door

LAERTES: I thank you: keep the door. O thou vile king,

Give me my father!

QUEEN GERTRUDE: Calmly, good Laertes.

LAERTES: That drop of blood that's calm proclaims me bastard,

Cries cuckold to my father, brands the harlot

Even here, between the chaste unsmirched brow

Of my true mother.

KING CLAUDIUS: What is the cause, Laertes,

That thy rebellion looks so giant-like?

Let him go, Gertrude; do not fear our person:

There's such divinity doth hedge a king,

That treason can but peep to what it would,

Acts little of his will. Tell me, Laertes,

Why thou art thus incensed. Let him go, Gertrude.

Speak, man.

LAERTES: Where is my father?

KING CLAUDIUS: Dead.

QUEEN GERTRUDE: But not by him.

KING CLAUDIUS: Let him demand his fill.

LAERTES: How came he dead? I'll not be juggled with:

To hell, allegiance! vows, to the blackest devil!

Conscience and grace, to the profoundest pit!

I dare damnation. To this point I stand,

That both the worlds I give to negligence,

Let come what comes; only I'll be revenged

Most thoroughly for my father.

KING CLAUDIUS: Who shall stay you?

LAERTES: My will, not all the world:

And for my means, I'll husband them so well,

They shall go far with little.

KING CLAUDIUS: Good Laertes,

If you desire to know the certainty

Of your dear father's death, is't writ in your revenge,

That, swoopstake, you will draw both friend and foe,

Winner and loser?

LAERTES: None but his enemies.

KING CLAUDIUS: Will you know them then?

LAERTES: To his good friends thus wide I'll ope my arms;

And like the kind life-rendering pelican,

Repast them with my blood.

KING CLAUDIUS: Why, now you speak

Like a good child and a true gentleman.

That I am guiltless of your father's death,

And am most sensible in grief for it,

It shall as level to your judgment pierce

As day does to your eye.

DANES: [Within] Let her come in.

LAERTES: How now! what noise is that?

[Re-enter OPHELIA]

O heat, dry up my brains! tears seven times salt,

Burn out the sense and virtue of mine eye!

By heaven, thy madness shall be paid by weight,

Till our scale turn the beam. O rose of May!

Dear maid, kind sister, sweet Ophelia!

O heavens! is't possible, a young maid's wits

Should be as moral as an old man's life?

Nature is fine in love, and where 'tis fine,

It sends some precious instance of itself

After the thing it loves.

OPHELIA: [Sings]   They bore him barefaced on the bier;

Hey non nonny, nonny, hey nonny;

And in his grave rain'd many a tear:—

Fare you well, my dove!

LAERTES: Hadst thou thy wits, and didst persuade revenge,

It could not move thus.

OPHELIA: [Sings]   You must sing a-down a-down,

An you call him a-down-a.

O, how the wheel becomes it! It is the false

steward, that stole his master's daughter.

LAERTES: This nothing's more than matter.

OPHELIA: There's rosemary, that's for remembrance; pray,

love, remember: and there is pansies. that's for thoughts.

LAERTES: A document[4] in madness, thoughts and remembrance fitted.

OPHELIA: There's fennel for you, and columbines: there's rue

for you; and here's some for me: we may call it

herb-grace o' Sundays: O you must wear your rue with

a difference. There's a daisy: I would give you

some violets, but they withered all when my father

died: they say he made a good end—

[Sings] For bonny sweet Robin is all my joy.

---

[4] lesson

LAERTES: Thought and affliction, passion, hell itself,

She turns to favour and to prettiness.

OPHELIA: [Sings]   And will he not come again?

   And will he not come again?

   No, no, he is dead:

     Go to thy death-bed:

   He never will come again.

     His beard was as white as snow,

   All flaxen was his poll:

     He is gone, he is gone,

   And we cast away moan:

     God ha' mercy on his soul!

And of all Christian souls, I pray God. God be wi' ye.

[Exit]

LAERTES: Do you see this, O God?

KING CLAUDIUS: Laertes, I must commune with your grief,

Or you deny me right. Go but apart,

Make choice of whom your wisest friends you will.

And they shall hear and judge 'twixt you and me:

If by direct or by collateral hand

They find us touch'd, we will our kingdom give,

Our crown, our life, and all that we can ours,

To you in satisfaction; but if not,

Be you content to lend your patience to us,

And we shall jointly labour with your soul

To give it due content.

LAERTES: Let this be so;

His means of death, his obscure funeral—

No trophy, sword, nor hatchment o'er his bones,

No noble rite nor formal ostentation—

Cry to be heard, as 'twere from heaven to earth,

That I must call't in question.

KING CLAUDIUS: So you shall;

And where the offence is let the great axe fall.

I pray you, go with me.

[Exeunt]

ACT IV: SCENE VI

SCENE VI. Another room in the castle.

[Enter HORATIO and a SERVANT]

HORATIO: What are they that would speak with me?

SERVANT: Sailors, sir: they say they have letters for you.

HORATIO: Let them come in.

[Exit Servant]

I do not know from what part of the world

I should be greeted, if not from Lord Hamlet.

[Enter Sailors]

FIRST SAILOR: God bless you, sir.

HORATIO: Let him bless thee too.

FIRST SAILOR: He shall, sir, an't please him. There's a letter for

you, sir; it comes from the ambassador that was

bound for England; if your name be Horatio, as I am

let to know it is.

HORATIO: [Reads] 'Horatio, when thou shalt have overlooked this, give these fellows some means to the king: they have letters for him. Ere we were two days old at sea, a pirate of very warlike appointment gave us chase. Finding ourselves too slow of sail, we put on a compelled valour, and in the grapple I boarded them: on the instant they got clear of our ship; so I alone became their prisoner. They have dealt with me like thieves of mercy: but they knew what they did; I am to do a good turn for them. Let the king have the letters I have sent; and repair thou to me with as much speed as thou wouldst fly death. I have words to speak in thine ear will make thee dumb; yet are they much too light for the bore[1] of the matter. These good fellows will bring thee where I am. Rosencrantz and Guildenstern hold their course for England: of them I have much to tell thee. Farewell. 'He that thou knowest thine, HAMLET.'

Come, I will make you way for these your letters;

And do't the speedier, that you may direct me

To him from whom you brought them.

[Exeunt]

---

[1] Heaviness

ACT IV: SCENE VII

SCENE VII. Another room in the castle.

[Enter KING CLAUDIUS and LAERTES]

KING CLAUDIUS: Now must your conscience my acquaintance seal,

And you must put me in your heart for friend,

Sith you have heard, and with a knowing ear,

That he which hath your noble father slain

Pursued my life.

LAERTES: It well appears: but tell me

Why you proceeded not against these feats,

So crimeful and so capital in nature,

As by your safety, wisdom, all things else,

You mainly[1] were stirr'd up.

KING CLAUDIUS: O, for two special reasons;

Which may to you, perhaps, seem much unsinew'd,

But yet to me they are strong. The queen his mother

Lives almost by his looks; and for myself—

My virtue or my plague, be it either which—

She's so conjunctive to my life and soul,

That, as the star moves not but in his sphere,

I could not but by her. The other motive,

Why to a public count I might not go,

Is the great love the general gender[2] bear him;

Who, dipping all his faults in their affection,

---

[1] Strongly

[2] Sort

Would, like the spring that turneth wood to stone,

Convert his gyves to graces; so that my arrows,

Too slightly timber'd for so loud a wind,

Would have reverted to my bow again,

And not where I had aim'd them.

LAERTES: And so have I a noble father lost;

A sister driven into desperate terms,

Whose worth, if praises may go back again,

Stood challenger on mount of all the age

For her perfections: but my revenge will come.

KING CLAUDIUS: Break not your sleeps for that: you must not think

That we are made of stuff so flat and dull

That we can let our beard be shook with danger

And think it pastime. You shortly shall hear more:

I loved your father, and we love ourself;

And that, I hope, will teach you to imagine—

[Enter a Messenger]

How now! what news?

MESSENGER: Letters, my lord, from Hamlet:

This to your majesty; this to the queen.

KING CLAUDIUS: From Hamlet! who brought them?

MESSENGER: Sailors, my lord, they say; I saw them not:

They were given me by Claudio; he received them

Of him that brought them.

KING CLAUDIUS: Laertes, you shall hear them. Leave us.

[Exit Messenger]

[Reads] 'High and mighty, You shall know I am set naked[3] on your kingdom. To-morrow shall I beg leave to see your kingly eyes: when I shall, first asking your pardon thereunto, recount the occasion of my sudden and more strange return.
  'HAMLET.'

What should this mean? Are all the rest come back?

Or is it some abuse[4], and no such thing?

LAERTES: Know you the hand?

KING CLAUDIUS: 'Tis Hamlets character. 'Naked!

And in a postscript here, he says 'alone.'

Can you advise me?

LAERTES: I'm lost in it, my lord. But let him come;

It warms the very sickness in my heart,

That I shall live and tell him to his teeth,

'Thus didest thou.'

KING CLAUDIUS: If it be so, Laertes—

As how should it be so? how otherwise?—

Will you be ruled by me?

LAERTES: Ay, my lord;

So you will not o'errule me to a peace.

KING CLAUDIUS: To thine own peace. If he be now return'd,

As checking at his voyage, and that he means

No more to undertake it, I will work him

To an exploit, now ripe in my device,

Under the which he shall not choose but fall:

And for his death no wind of blame shall breathe,

But even his mother shall uncharge the practise[5]

[3] Alone (Hudson)

[4] Deception

[5] Call him blameless

And call it accident.

LAERTES: My lord, I will be ruled;

The rather, if you could devise it so

That I might be the organ.

KING CLAUDIUS: It falls right.

You have been talk'd of since your travel much,

And that in Hamlet's hearing, for a quality

Wherein, they say, you shine: your sum of parts

Did not together pluck such envy from him

As did that one, and that, in my regard,

Of the unworthiest siege.

LAERTES: What part is that, my lord?

KING CLAUDIUS: A very riband in the cap of youth,

Yet needful too; for youth no less becomes

The light and careless livery that it wears

Than settled age his sables and his weeds,

Importing health and graveness. Two months since,

Here was a gentleman of Normandy:—

I've seen myself, and served against, the French,

And they can well on horseback: but this gallant

Had witchcraft in't; he grew unto his seat;

And to such wondrous doing brought his horse,

As he had been incorpsed and demi-natured

With the brave beast: so far he topp'd my thought,

That I, in forgery of shapes and tricks,

Come short of what he did.

LAERTES: A Norman was't?

KING CLAUDIUS: A Norman.

LAERTES: Upon my life, Lamond.

KING CLAUDIUS: The very same.

LAERTES: I know him well: he is the brooch indeed

And gem of all the nation.

KING CLAUDIUS: He made confession of you,

And gave you such a masterly report

For art and exercise in your defence[6]

And for your rapier most especially,

That he cried out, 'twould be a sight indeed,

If one could match you: the scrimers[7] of their nation,

He swore, had had neither motion, guard, nor eye,

If you opposed them. Sir, this report of his

Did Hamlet so envenom with his envy[8]

That he could nothing do but wish and beg

Your sudden coming o'er, to play with him.

Now, out of this,—

LAERTES: What out of this, my lord?

KING CLAUDIUS: Laertes, was your father dear to you?

Or are you like the painting of a sorrow,

A face without a heart?

LAERTES: Why ask you this?

KING CLAUDIUS: Not that I think you did not love your father;

But that I know love is begun by time;

And that I see, in passages of proof,

---

[6] Praise

[7] Fencers

[8] Make him (Hamlet) jealous

Time qualifies the spark and fire of it.

There lives within the very flame of love

A kind of wick or snuff that will abate it;

And nothing is at a like goodness still;

For goodness, growing to a plurisy,

Dies in his own too much: that we would do

We should do when we would; for this 'would' changes

And hath abatements and delays as many

As there are tongues, are hands, are accidents;

And then this 'should' is like a spendthrift sigh,

That hurts by easing. But, to the quick o' the ulcer:—

Hamlet comes back: what would you undertake,

To show yourself your father's son in deed

More than in words?

LAERTES: To cut his throat i' the church.

KING CLAUDIUS: No place, indeed, should murder sanctuarize[9];

Revenge should have no bounds. But, good Laertes,

Will you do this, keep close within your chamber.

Hamlet return'd shall know you are come home:

We'll put on those shall praise your excellence

And set a double varnish on the fame

The Frenchman gave you, bring you in fine together

And wager on your heads: he, being remiss,

Most generous and free from all contriving,

Will not peruse the foils; so that, with ease,

Or with a little shuffling, you may choose

A sword unbated, and in a pass of practise

---

[9] He (Hamlet) should have no sanctuary from murder

Requite[10] him for your father.

LAERTES: I will do't:

And, for that purpose, I'll anoint my sword.

I bought an unction of a mountebank,

So mortal that, but dip a knife in it,

Where it draws blood no cataplasm so rare,

Collected from all simples that have virtue

Under the moon, can save the thing from death

That is but scratch'd withal: I'll touch my point

With this contagion, that, if I gall him slightly,

It may be death.

KING CLAUDIUS: Let's further think of this;

Weigh what convenience both of time and means

May fit us to our shape: if this should fail,

And that our drift look through our bad performance,

'Twere better not assay'd[11]: therefore this project

Should have a back or second, that might hold,

If this should blast in proof. Soft! let me see:

We'll make a solemn wager on your cunnings: I ha't.

When in your motion you are hot and dry—

As make your bouts more violent to that end—

And that he calls for drink, I'll have prepared him

A chalice for the nonce, whereon but sipping,

If he by chance escape your venom'd stuck,

Our purpose may hold there.

---

[10] Avenge

[11] It would be better that we didn't try this at all if we don't get it right, so let's have a back up plan

[Enter QUEEN GERTRUDE]

How now, sweet queen!

QUEEN GERTRUDE: One woe doth tread upon another's heel,

So fast they follow; your sister's drown'd, Laertes.

LAERTES: Drown'd! O, where?

QUEEN GERTRUDE: There is a willow grows aslant a brook,

That shows his hoar leaves in the glassy stream;

There with fantastic garlands did she come

Of crow-flowers, nettles, daisies, and long purples

That liberal shepherds give a grosser name,

But our cold maids do dead men's fingers call them:

There, on the pendent boughs her coronet weeds

Clambering to hang, an envious sliver broke;

When down her weedy trophies and herself

Fell in the weeping brook. Her clothes spread wide;

And, mermaid-like, awhile they bore her up:

Which time she chanted snatches of old tunes;

As one incapable of her own distress,

Or like a creature native and indued

Unto that element: but long it could not be

Till that her garments, heavy with their drink,

Pull'd the poor wretch from her melodious lay

To muddy death.

LAERTES: Alas, then, she is drown'd?

QUEEN GERTRUDE: Drown'd, drown'd.

LAERTES: Too much of water hast thou, poor Ophelia,

And therefore I forbid my tears: but yet

It is our trick; nature her custom holds,

Let shame say what it will: when these are gone,

The woman will be out[12]. Adieu, my lord:

I have a speech of fire, that fain would blaze,

But that this folly doubts it.

[Exit]

KING CLAUDIUS: Let's follow, Gertrude:

How much I had to do to calm his rage!

Now fear I this will give it start again;

Therefore let's follow.

[Exeunt]

---

[12] The womanly part of me ("my tears") (see Hudson)

ACT V SUMMARY

Act V begins in the burial ground, where a pair of gravediggers make light of their duty. Hamlet and Horatio chat with them a bit before they are interrupted by Ophelia's funeral procession. When Hamlet realizes that Ophelia has died, he reveals that he has returned and loudly mourns her death. Laertes attempts to fight with him briefly but he is pulled away.

Later, Hamlet tells Horatio how he managed to escape from his voyage to England. At some point he realized that Claudius had planned to have him killed en route, but he was able to trick Rosencrantz and Guildenstern into being killed in his place. He feels no remorse over this.

Shortly thereafter, a courtier arrives to inform Hamlet of Laertes' invitation to a fencing match. Hamlet accepts, and although Horatio has misgivings about the fight, Hamlet tells him not to worry. He explains that his experience with divine Providence has taught him that all things must follow the course of their own fate, and that there is no use in trying to alter one's destiny.

Laertes and Hamlet meet to begin their fight once and for all. Before they begin, Hamlet apologizes to Laertes at having accidentally killed his father Polonius, and Laertes appears to accept. While dueling, Laertes scratches Hamlet with the poisoned tip of his sword. Their swords then fall and become switched, allowing Hamlet to also scratch Laertes with the same poisoned sword. Meanwhile, the poisoned wine that Claudius has meant to save for Hamlet is accidentally drunk by Gertrude, leading to her instant death. Upon realizing what's happening, Hamlet stabs his uncle, finally achieving the revenge he has worked so hard for.

As everyone dies, Hamlet tells Horatio to remember what he has seen and relay his tale to the world. Fortinbras arrives at the end of this bloody fray and assumes command of the crown of Denmark.

ACT V: SCENE I

SCENE I. A churchyard.

[Enter two Clowns, with spades, etc]

FIRST CLOWN: Is she to be buried in Christian burial that

wilfully seeks her own salvation?

SECOND CLOWN: I tell thee she is: and therefore make her grave

straight: the crowner hath sat on her, and finds it

Christian burial.

FIRST CLOWN: How can that be, unless she drowned herself in her

own defence?

SECOND CLOWN: Why, 'tis found so.

FIRST CLOWN: It must be 'se offendendo;[1] it cannot be else. For

here lies the point: if I drown myself wittingly,

it argues an act: and an act hath three branches: it

is, to act, to do, to perform: argal[2], she drowned

herself wittingly.

SECOND CLOWN: Nay, but hear you, goodman delver,—

FIRST CLOWN: Give me leave. Here lies the water; good: here

stands the man; good; if the man go to this water,

and drown himself, it is, will he, nill he, he

goes,—mark you that; but if the water come to him

and drown him, he drowns not himself: argal, he

---

[1] A joke; these two are going back and forth about Ophelia's death as a suicide. The joke is that her death must have been committed in "self offense" (rather than self defense)

[2] ergo; it's a common Shakespearean trope for uneducated characters to botch the use of "high speech"

that is not guilty of his own death shortens not his own life.

SECOND CLOWN: But is this law?

FIRST CLOWN: Ay, marry, is't; crowner's quest law.

SECOND CLOWN: Will you ha' the truth on't? If this had not been

a gentlewoman, she should have been buried out o'

Christian burial.

FIRST CLOWN: Why, there thou say'st: and the more pity that

great folk should have countenance in this world to

drown or hang themselves, more than their even

Christian. Come, my spade. There is no ancient

gentleman but gardeners, ditchers, and grave-makers:

they hold up Adam's profession.

SECOND CLOWN: Was he a gentleman?

FIRST CLOWN: He was the first that ever bore arms.

SECOND CLOWN: Why, he had none.

FIRST CLOWN: What, art a heathen? How dost thou understand the

Scripture? The Scripture says 'Adam digged:'

could he dig without arms? I'll put another

question to thee: if thou answerest me not to the

purpose, confess thyself—

SECOND CLOWN: Go to.

FIRST CLOWN: What is he that builds stronger than either the

mason, the shipwright, or the carpenter?

SECOND CLOWN: The gallows-maker; for that frame outlives a

thousand tenants.

FIRST CLOWN: I like thy wit well, in good faith: the gallows

does well; but how does it well? it does well to

those that do in: now thou dost ill to say the

gallows is built stronger than the church: argal,

the gallows may do well to thee. To't again, come.

SECOND CLOWN: 'Who builds stronger than a mason, a shipwright, or

a carpenter?'

FIRST CLOWN: Ay, tell me that, and unyoke.

SECOND CLOWN: Marry, now I can tell.

FIRST CLOWN: To't.

SECOND CLOWN: Mass, I cannot tell.

[Enter HAMLET and HORATIO, at a distance]

FIRST CLOWN: Cudgel thy brains no more about it, for your dull

ass will not mend his pace with beating; and, when

you are asked this question next, say 'a

grave-maker: 'the houses that he makes last till

doomsday. Go, get thee to Yaughan: fetch me a

stoup of liquor.

[Exit Second Clown]

He digs and sings

In youth, when I did love, did love,

Methought it was very sweet,

To contract, O, the time, for, ah, my behove,

O, methought, there was nothing meet.

HAMLET: Has this fellow no feeling of his business, that he

sings at grave-making?

HORATIO: Custom hath made it in him a property of easiness.

HAMLET: 'Tis e'en so: the hand of little employment hath

the daintier sense.

FIRST CLOWN: [Sings]   But age, with his stealing steps,

Hath claw'd me in his clutch,

And hath shipped me into the land,

As if I had never been such.

[Throws up a skull]

HAMLET: That skull had a tongue in it, and could sing once:

how the knave jowls it to the ground, as if it were

Cain's jaw-bone, that did the first murder! It

might be the pate of a politician, which this ass

now o'er-reaches; one that would circumvent God,

might it not?

HORATIO: It might, my lord.

HAMLET: Or of a courtier; which could say 'Good morrow,

sweet lord! How dost thou, good lord?' This might

be my lord such-a-one, that praised my lord

such-a-one's horse, when he meant to beg it; might it not?

HORATIO: Ay, my lord.

HAMLET: Why, e'en so: and now my Lady Worm's[3]; chapless, and

knocked about the mazzard with a sexton's spade:

here's fine revolution, an we had the trick to

see't. Did these bones cost no more the breeding,

but to play at loggats with 'em? mine ache to think on't.

FIRST CLOWN: [Sings] A pick-axe, and a spade, a spade,

For and a shrouding sheet:

O, a pit of clay for to be made

For such a guest is meet.

[Throws up another skull]

HAMLET: There's another: why may not that be the skull of a

lawyer? Where be his quiddities now, his quillets,

---

[3] ie, Lady So-and-So

his cases, his tenures, and his tricks? why does he
suffer this rude knave now to knock him about the
sconce with a dirty shovel, and will not tell him of
his action of battery? Hum! This fellow might be
in's time a great buyer of land, with his statutes,
his recognizances, his fines, his double vouchers,
his recoveries: is this the fine of his fines, and
the recovery of his recoveries, to have his fine
pate full of fine dirt?[4] will his vouchers vouch him
no more of his purchases, and double ones too, than
the length and breadth of a pair of indentures? The
very conveyances of his lands will hardly lie in
this box; and must the inheritor himself have no more, ha?

HORATIO: Not a jot more, my lord.

HAMLET: Is not parchment made of sheepskins?

HORATIO: Ay, my lord, and of calf-skins too.

HAMLET: They are sheep and calves which seek out assurance
in that. I will speak to this fellow. Whose
grave's this, sirrah?

FIRST CLOWN: Mine, sir.

　　　　[Sings] O, a pit of clay for to be made
　　　　　　　　For such a guest is meet.

HAMLET: I think it be thine, indeed; for thou liest in't.

FIRST CLOWN: You lie out on't, sir, and therefore it is not
yours: for my part, I do not lie in't, and yet it is mine.

HAMLET: 'Thou dost lie in't, to be in't and say it is thine:

---

4 Much of this is a lengthy pun on the nature of life and jobs and lawyers and fines and
infinity (see Hudson)

'tis for the dead, not for the quick; therefore thou liest.

FIRST CLOWN: 'Tis a quick lie, sir; 'twill away gain, from me to

you.

HAMLET: What man dost thou dig it for?

FIRST CLOWN: For no man, sir.

HAMLET: What woman, then?

FIRST CLOWN: For none, neither.

HAMLET: Who is to be buried in't?

FIRST CLOWN: One that was a woman, sir; but, rest her soul, she's dead.

HAMLET: How absolute the knave is! we must speak by the

card[5], or equivocation will undo us. By the Lord,

Horatio, these three years I have taken a note of

it; the age is grown so picked that the toe of the

peasant comes so near the heel of the courtier, he

gaffs his kibe. How long hast thou been a

grave-maker?

FIRST CLOWN: Of all the days i' the year, I came to't that day

that our last king Hamlet overcame Fortinbras.

HAMLET: How long is that since?

FIRST CLOWN: Cannot you tell that? every fool can tell that: it

was the very day that young Hamlet was born; he that

is mad, and sent into England.

HAMLET: Ay, marry, why was he sent into England?

FIRST CLOWN: Why, because he was mad: he shall recover his wits

there; or, if he do not, it's no great matter there.

HAMLET: Why?

---

[5] very explicitly

FIRST CLOWN: 'Twill, a not be seen in him there; there the men

are as mad as he.

HAMLET: How came he mad?

FIRST CLOWN: Very strangely, they say.

HAMLET: How strangely?

FIRST CLOWN: Faith, e'en with losing his wits.

HAMLET: Upon what ground?

FIRST CLOWN: Why, here in Denmark: I have been sexton here, man

and boy, thirty years.

HAMLET: How long will a man lie i' the earth ere he rot?

FIRST CLOWN: I' faith, if he be not rotten before he die—as we

have many pocky corses now-a-days, that will scarce

hold the laying in—he will last you some eight year

or nine year: a tanner will last you nine year.

HAMLET: Why he more than another?

FIRST CLOWN: Why, sir, his hide is so tanned with his trade, that

he will keep out water a great while; and your water

is a sore decayer of your whoreson dead body.

Here's a skull now; this skull has lain in the earth

three and twenty years.

HAMLET: Whose was it?

FIRST CLOWN: A whoreson mad fellow's it was: whose do you think it was?

HAMLET: Nay, I know not.

FIRST CLOWN: A pestilence on him for a mad rogue! a' poured a

flagon of Rhenish on my head once. This same skull,

sir, was Yorick's skull, the king's jester.

HAMLET: This?

FIRST CLOWN: E'en that.

HAMLET: Let me see.

[Takes the skull]

Alas, poor Yorick! I knew him, Horatio: a fellow

of infinite jest, of most excellent fancy: he hath

borne me on his back a thousand times; and now, how

abhorred in my imagination it is! my gorge rims at

it. Here hung those lips that I have kissed I know

not how oft. Where be your gibes now? your

gambols? your songs? your flashes of merriment,

that were wont to set the table on a roar? Not one

now, to mock your own grinning? quite chap-fallen?

Now get you to my lady's chamber, and tell her, let

her paint an inch thick, to this favour she must

come; make her laugh at that. Prithee, Horatio, tell

me one thing.

HORATIO: What's that, my lord?

HAMLET: Dost thou think Alexander looked o' this fashion i'

the earth?

HORATIO: E'en so.

HAMLET: And smelt so? pah!

[Puts down the skull]

HORATIO: E'en so, my lord.

HAMLET: To what base uses we may return, Horatio! Why may

not imagination trace the noble dust of Alexander,

till he find it stopping a bung-hole?

HORATIO: 'Twere to consider too curiously, to consider so.

HAMLET: No, faith, not a jot; but to follow him thither with modesty enough, and likelihood to lead it: as

thus: Alexander died, Alexander was buried,

Alexander returneth into dust; the dust is earth; of

earth we make loam; and why of that loam, whereto he

was converted, might they not stop a beer-barrel?

Imperious Caesar, dead and turn'd to clay,

Might stop a hole to keep the wind away:

O, that that earth, which kept the world in awe,

Should patch a wall to expel the winter flaw!

But soft! but soft! aside: here comes the king.

[Enter Priest, etc. in procession; the Corpse of OPHELIA, LAERTES and Mourners following; KING CLAUDIUS, QUEEN GERTRUDE, their trains, etc]

The queen, the courtiers: who is this they follow?

And with such maimed rites? This doth betoken

The corse they follow did with desperate hand

Fordo its own life: 'twas of some estate.

Couch we awhile, and mark.

[Retiring with HORATIO]

LAERTES: What ceremony else?

HAMLET: That is Laertes,

A very noble youth: mark.

LAERTES: What ceremony else?

FIRST PRIEST: Her obsequies have been as far enlarged

As we have warrantise: her death was doubtful;

And, but that great command o'ersways the order,

She should in ground unsanctified have lodged

Till the last trumpet: for charitable prayers,

Shards, flints and pebbles should be thrown on her;

Yet here she is allow'd her virgin crants[6],

Her maiden strewments and the bringing home

Of bell and burial.

LAERTES: Must there no more be done?

FIRST PRIEST: No more be done:

We should profane the service of the dead

To sing a requiem and such rest to her

As to peace-parted souls.

LAERTES: Lay her i' the earth:

And from her fair and unpolluted flesh

May violets spring! I tell thee, churlish priest,

A ministering angel shall my sister be,

When thou liest howling.

HAMLET: What, the fair Ophelia!

QUEEN GERTRUDE: Sweets to the sweet: farewell!

[Scattering flowers]

I hoped thou shouldst have been my Hamlet's wife;

I thought thy bride-bed to have deck'd, sweet maid,

And not have strew'd thy grave.

LAERTES: O, treble woe

Fall ten times treble on that cursed head,

Whose wicked deed thy most ingenious sense

Deprived thee of! Hold off the earth awhile,

Till I have caught her once more in mine arms:

---

[6] Her virginal funeral ceremonies; Again, this tension of whether or not Ophelia deserves a Christian burial is continued

[Leaps into the grave]

Now pile your dust upon the quick and dead,

Till of this flat a mountain you have made,

To o'ertop old Pelion, or the skyish head

Of blue Olympus.

HAMLET: [Advancing] What is he whose grief

Bears such an emphasis? whose phrase of sorrow

Conjures the wandering stars, and makes them stand

Like wonder-wounded hearers? This is I,

Hamlet the Dane.

[Leaps into the grave]

LAERTES: The devil take thy soul!

[Grappling with him]

HAMLET: Thou pray'st not well.

I prithee, take thy fingers from my throat;

For, though I am not splenitive and rash,

Yet have I something in me dangerous,

Which let thy wiseness fear: hold off thy hand.

KING CLAUDIUS: Pluck them asunder.

QUEEN GERTRUDE: Hamlet, Hamlet!

ALL: Gentlemen—!

HORATIO: Good my lord, be quiet.

[Hamlet and Laertes are parted]

HAMLET: Why I will fight with him upon this theme

Until my eyelids will no longer wag.

QUEEN GERTRUDE: O my son, what theme?

HAMLET: I loved Ophelia: forty thousand brothers

Could not, with all their quantity of love,

Make up my sum. What wilt thou do for her?

KING CLAUDIUS: O, he is mad, Laertes.

QUEEN GERTRUDE: For love of God, forbear him.

HAMLET: 'Swounds, show me what thou'lt do:

Woo't[7] weep? woo't fight? woo't fast? woo't tear thyself?

Woo't drink up eisel? eat a crocodile?

I'll do't. Dost thou come here to whine?

To outface me with leaping in her grave?

Be buried quick with her, and so will I:

And, if thou prate of mountains, let them throw

Millions of acres on us, till our ground,

Singeing his pate against the burning zone,

Make Ossa like a wart! Nay, an thou'lt mouth,

I'll rant as well as thou.

QUEEN GERTRUDE: This is mere madness:

And thus awhile the fit will work on him;

Anon, as patient as the female dove,

When that her golden couplets are disclosed,

His silence will sit drooping.

HAMLET: Hear you, sir;

What is the reason that you use me thus?

I loved you ever: but it is no matter;

Let Hercules himself do what he may,

The cat will mew and dog will have his day.

[Exit]

KING CLAUDIUS: I pray you, good Horatio, wait upon him.

[Exit HORATIO]

---

[7] Would; Again, Hamlet is ranting and raving in the throes of his passion and distress

[To LAERTES] Strengthen your patience in our last night's speech;

We'll put the matter to the present push.

Good Gertrude, set some watch over your son.

This grave shall have a living monument:

An hour of quiet shortly shall we see;

Till then, in patience our proceeding be.

[Exeunt]

ACT V: SCENE II

SCENE II. A hall in the castle.

[Enter HAMLET and HORATIO]

HAMLET: So much for this, sir: now shall you see the other;

You do remember all the circumstance?

HORATIO: Remember it, my lord?

HAMLET: Sir, in my heart there was a kind of fighting,

That would not let me sleep: methought I lay

Worse than the mutines in the bilboes. Rashly,

And praised be rashness for it, let us know,

Our indiscretion sometimes serves us well,

When our deep plots do pall: and that should teach us

There's a divinity that shapes our ends,

Rough-hew them how we will—

HORATIO: That is most certain.

HAMLET: Up from my cabin,

My sea-gown scarf'd about me, in the dark

Groped I to find out them; had my desire.

Finger'd their packet, and in fine withdrew

To mine own room again; making so bold,

My fears forgetting manners, to unseal

Their grand commission; where I found, Horatio—

O royal knavery!—an exact command,

Larded with many several sorts of reasons

Importing Denmark's health and England's too,

With, ho! such bugs and goblins in my life,

That, on the supervise, no leisure bated,

No, not to stay the grinding of the axe,

My head should be struck off.

HORATIO: Is't possible?

HAMLET: Here's the commission: read it at more leisure.

But wilt thou hear me how I did proceed?

HORATIO: I beseech you.

HAMLET: Being thus be-netted round with villanies,—

Ere I could make a prologue to my brains,

They had begun the play—I sat me down,

Devised a new commission, wrote it fair:

I once did hold it, as our statists do,

A baseness to write fair and labour'd much

How to forget that learning, but, sir, now

It did me yeoman's service: wilt thou know

The effect of what I wrote?

HORATIO: Ay, good my lord.

HAMLET: An earnest conjuration from the king,

As England was his faithful tributary,

As love between them like the palm might flourish,

As peace should stiff her wheaten garland wear

And stand a comma 'tween their amities,

And many such-like 'As'es[1] of great charge,

That, on the view and knowing of these contents,

Without debatement further, more or less,

He should the bearers put to sudden death,

Not shriving-time allow'd.

---

[1] Repetition of "as" in the lines previous

HORATIO: How was this seal'd?

HAMLET: Why, even in that was heaven ordinant.

I had my father's signet in my purse,

Which was the model of that Danish seal;

Folded the writ up in form of the other,

Subscribed it, gave't the impression, placed it safely,

The changeling never known. Now, the next day

Was our sea-fight; and what to this was sequent

Thou know'st already.

HORATIO: So Guildenstern and Rosencrantz go to't[2].

HAMLET: Why, man, they did make love to this employment[3];

They are not near my conscience[4]; their defeat

Does by their own insinuation grow:

'Tis dangerous when the baser nature comes

Between the pass and fell incensed points

Of mighty opposites.

HORATIO: Why, what a king is this!

HAMLET: Does it not, think'st thee, stand me now upon—

He that hath kill'd my king and whored my mother,

Popp'd in between the election and my hopes,

Thrown out his angle for my proper life,

And with such cozenage—is't not perfect conscience,

To quit him with this arm? and is't not to be damn'd,

To let this canker of our nature come

---

2 go to it; ie, they went to their fates — they were killed

3 "They were willing participants in the plot against me and knew what they were getting into."

4 "I'm not concerned with them; they got what they deserved."

In further evil?

HORATIO: It must be shortly known to him from England

What is the issue of the business there.

HAMLET: It will be short: the interim is mine;

And a man's life's no more than to say 'One.'

But I am very sorry, good Horatio,

That to Laertes I forgot myself;

For, by the image of my cause, I see

The portraiture of his: I'll court his favours.

But, sure, the bravery of his grief did put me

Into a towering passion.

HORATIO: Peace! who comes here?

[Enter OSRIC]

OSRIC: Your lordship is right welcome back to Denmark.

HAMLET: I humbly thank you, sir. Dost know this water-fly?

HORATIO: No, my good lord.

HAMLET: Thy state is the more gracious; for 'tis a vice to

know him. He hath much land, and fertile: let a

beast be lord of beasts, and his crib shall stand at

the king's mess: 'tis a chough; but, as I say,

spacious in the possession of dirt.

OSRIC: Sweet lord, if your lordship were at leisure, I

should impart a thing to you from his majesty.

HAMLET: I will receive it, sir, with all diligence of

spirit. Put your bonnet to his right use; 'tis for the head.

OSRIC: I thank your lordship, it is very hot.

HAMLET: No, believe me, 'tis very cold; the wind is

northerly.

OSRIC: It is indifferent cold, my lord, indeed.

HAMLET: But yet methinks it is very sultry and hot for my

complexion.

OSRIC: Exceedingly, my lord; it is very sultry,—as

'twere,—I cannot tell how. But, my lord, his

majesty bade me signify to you that he has laid a

great wager on your head: sir, this is the matter,—

HAMLET: I beseech you, remember—5

[HAMLET moves him to put on his hat]

OSRIC: Nay, good my lord; for mine ease, in good faith.

Sir, here is newly come to court Laertes; believe

me, an absolute gentleman, full of most excellent

differences, of very soft society and great showing:

indeed, to speak feelingly of him, he is the card or

calendar of gentry, for you shall find in him the

continent of what part a gentleman would see.

HAMLET: Sir, his definement suffers no perdition in you;

though, I know, to divide him inventorially would

dizzy the arithmetic of memory, and yet but yaw

neither, in respect of his quick sail. But, in the

verity of extolment, I take him to be a soul of

great article; and his infusion of such dearth and

rareness, as, to make true diction of him, his

semblable is his mirror; and who else would trace

him, his umbrage, nothing more.

OSRIC: Your lordship speaks most infallibly of him.

HAMLET: The concernancy, sir? why do we wrap the gentleman

---

5 Hamlet is chiding him for failing to return his cap to his head as a sign of respect

in our more rawer breath?

OSRIC: Sir?

HORATIO: Is't not possible to understand in another tongue?

You will do't, sir, really.

HAMLET: What imports the nomination of this gentleman?

OSRIC: Of Laertes?

HORATIO: His purse is empty already; all's golden words are spent.

HAMLET: Of him, sir.

OSRIC: I know you are not ignorant—

HAMLET: I would you did, sir; yet, in faith, if you did,

it would not much approve me. Well, sir?

OSRIC: You are not ignorant of what excellence Laertes is—

HAMLET: I dare not confess that, lest I should compare with

him in excellence; but, to know a man well, were to

know himself.

OSRIC: I mean, sir, for his weapon; but in the imputation

laid on him by them, in his meed he's unfellowed.

HAMLET: What's his weapon?

OSRIC: Rapier and dagger.

HAMLET: That's two of his weapons: but, well—

OSRIC: The king, sir, hath wagered with him six Barbary

horses: against the which he has imponed[6], as I take

it, six French rapiers and poniards, with their

assigns, as girdle, hangers, and so: three of the

carriages, in faith, are very dear to fancy, very

responsive to the hilts, most delicate carriages,

---

[6] wagered

and of very liberal conceit.

HAMLET: What call you the carriages?

HORATIO: I knew you must be edified by the margent ere you had done.

OSRIC: The carriages, sir, are the hangers.

HAMLET: The phrase would be more german to the matter, if we
could carry cannon by our sides: I would it might
be hangers till then. But, on: six Barbary horses
against six French swords, their assigns, and three
liberal-conceited carriages; that's the French bet
against the Danish. Why is this 'imponed,' as you call it?

OSRIC: The king, sir, hath laid, that in a dozen passes
between yourself and him, he shall not exceed you
three hits: he hath laid on twelve for nine; and it
would come to immediate trial, if your lordship
would vouchsafe the answer.

HAMLET: How if I answer 'no'?

OSRIC: I mean, my lord, the opposition of your person in trial.

HAMLET: Sir, I will walk here in the hall: if it please his
majesty, 'tis the breathing time of day with me; let
the foils be brought, the gentleman willing, and the
king hold his purpose, I will win for him an I can;
if not, I will gain nothing but my shame and the odd hits.

OSRIC: Shall I re-deliver you e'en so?

HAMLET: To this effect, sir; after what flourish your nature will.

OSRIC: I commend my duty to your lordship.

HAMLET: Yours, yours.

[Exit OSRIC]

He does well to commend it himself; there are no

tongues else for's turn.

HORATIO: This lapwing runs away with the shell on his head.

HAMLET: He did comply with his dug, before he sucked it.
Thus has he—and many more of the same bevy that I
know the dressy age dotes on—only got the tune of
the time and outward habit of encounter; a kind of
yesty collection, which carries them through and
through the most fond and winnowed opinions; and do
but blow them to their trial, the bubbles are out.

[Enter a Lord]

LORD: My lord, his majesty commended him to you by young
Osric, who brings back to him that you attend him in
the hall: he sends to know if your pleasure hold to
play with Laertes, or that you will take longer time.

HAMLET: I am constant to my purpose; they follow the king's
pleasure: if his fitness speaks, mine is ready; now
or whensoever, provided I be so able as now.

LORD: The king and queen and all are coming down.

HAMLET: In happy time.

LORD: The queen desires you to use some gentle
entertainment to Laertes before you fall to play.

HAMLET: She well instructs me.

[Exit Lord]

HORATIO: You will lose this wager, my lord.

HAMLET: I do not think so: since he went into France, I
have been in continual practise: I shall win at the
odds. But thou wouldst not think how ill all's here
about my heart: but it is no matter.

HORATIO: Nay, good my lord,—

HAMLET: It is but foolery; but it is such a kind of

gain-giving, as would perhaps trouble a woman.

HORATIO: If your mind dislike any thing, obey it: I will

forestall their repair hither, and say you are not

fit.

HAMLET: Not a whit, we defy augury: there's a special

providence in the fall of a sparrow. If it be now,

'tis not to come; if it be not to come, it will be

now; if it be not now, yet it will come: the

readiness is all: since no man has aught of what he

leaves, what is't to leave betimes? Let be.

[Enter KING CLAUDIUS, QUEEN GERTRUDE, LAERTES, Lords,
OSRIC, and Attendants with foils.]

KING CLAUDIUS: Come, Hamlet, come, and take this hand from me.

[KING CLAUDIUS puts LAERTES' hand into HAMLET's]

HAMLET: Give me your pardon, sir: I've done you wrong;

But pardon't, as you are a gentleman.

This presence knows,

And you must needs have heard, how I am punish'd

With sore distraction. What I have done,

That might your nature, honour and exception

Roughly awake, I here proclaim was madness.

Was't Hamlet wrong'd Laertes? Never Hamlet:

If Hamlet from himself be ta'en away,

And when he's not himself does wrong Laertes,

Then Hamlet does it not, Hamlet denies it.

Who does it, then? His madness: if't be so,

Hamlet is of the faction that is wrong'd;

His madness is poor Hamlet's enemy.

Sir, in this audience,

Let my disclaiming from a purposed evil

Free me so far in your most generous thoughts,

That I have shot mine arrow o'er the house,

And hurt my brother.

LAERTES: I am satisfied in nature,

Whose motive, in this case, should stir me most

To my revenge: but in my terms of honour

I stand aloof; and will no reconcilement,

Till by some elder masters, of known honour,

I have a voice and precedent of peace,

To keep my name ungored. But till that time,

I do receive your offer'd love like love,

And will not wrong it.

HAMLET: I embrace it freely;

And will this brother's wager frankly play.

Give us the foils. Come on.

LAERTES: Come, one for me.

HAMLET: I'll be your foil, Laertes: in mine ignorance

Your skill shall, like a star i' the darkest night,

Stick fiery off indeed.

LAERTES: You mock me, sir.

HAMLET: No, by this hand.

KING CLAUDIUS: Give them the foils, young Osric. Cousin Hamlet,

You know the wager?

HAMLET: Very well, my lord

Your grace hath laid the odds o' the weaker side.

KING CLAUDIUS: I do not fear it; I have seen you both:

But since he is better'd, we have therefore odds.

LAERTES: This is too heavy, let me see another.

HAMLET: This likes me well. These foils have all a length?

[They prepare to play]

OSRIC: Ay, my good lord.

KING CLAUDIUS: Set me the stoops of wine upon that table.

If Hamlet give the first or second hit,

Or quit in answer of the third exchange,

Let all the battlements their ordnance fire:

The king shall drink to Hamlet's better breath;

And in the cup an union shall he throw,

Richer than that which four successive kings

In Denmark's crown have worn. Give me the cups;

And let the kettle to the trumpet speak,

The trumpet to the cannoneer without,

The cannons to the heavens, the heavens to earth,

'Now the king dunks to Hamlet.' Come, begin:

And you, the judges, bear a wary eye.

HAMLET: Come on, sir.

LAERTES: Come, my lord.

[They play]

HAMLET: One.

LAERTES: No.

HAMLET: Judgment.

OSRIC: A hit, a very palpable hit.

LAERTES: Well; again.

KING CLAUDIUS: Stay; give me drink. Hamlet, this pearl is thine;

Here's to thy health.

Trumpets sound, and cannon shot off within

Give him the cup.

HAMLET: I'll play this bout first; set it by awhile. Come.

[They play]

Another hit; what say you?

LAERTES: A touch, a touch, I do confess.

KING CLAUDIUS: Our son shall win.

QUEEN GERTRUDE: He's fat, and scant of breath.

Here, Hamlet, take my napkin, rub thy brows;

The queen carouses to thy fortune, Hamlet.

HAMLET: Good madam!

KING CLAUDIUS: Gertrude, do not drink.

QUEEN GERTRUDE: I will, my lord; I pray you, pardon me.

KING CLAUDIUS: [Aside] It is the poison'd cup: it is too late.

HAMLET: I dare not drink yet, madam; by and by.

QUEEN GERTRUDE: Come, let me wipe thy face.

LAERTES: My lord, I'll hit him now.

KING CLAUDIUS: I do not think't.

LAERTES: [Aside] And yet 'tis almost 'gainst my conscience.

HAMLET: Come, for the third, Laertes: you but dally;

I pray you, pass with your best violence;

I am afeard you make a wanton of me.

LAERTES: Say you so? come on.

[They play]

OSRIC: Nothing, neither way.

LAERTES: Have at you now!

***[LAERTES wounds HAMLET; then in scuffling, they change rapiers,
and HAMLET wounds LAERTES]***

KING CLAUDIUS: Part them; they are incensed.

HAMLET: Nay, come, again.

[QUEEN GERTRUDE falls]

OSRIC: Look to the queen there, ho!

HORATIO: They bleed on both sides. How is it, my lord?

OSRIC: How is't, Laertes?

LAERTES: Why, as a woodcock to mine own springe, Osric;

I am justly kill'd with mine own treachery.

HAMLET: How does the queen?

KING CLAUDIUS: She swounds to see them bleed.

QUEEN GERTRUDE: No, no, the drink, the drink,—O my dear Hamlet,—

The drink, the drink! I am poison'd.

[Dies]

HAMLET: O villany! Ho! let the door be lock'd:

Treachery! Seek it out.

LAERTES: It is here, Hamlet: Hamlet, thou art slain;

No medicine in the world can do thee good;

In thee there is not half an hour of life;

The treacherous instrument is in thy hand,

Unbated and envenom'd: the foul practise

Hath turn'd itself on me lo, here I lie,

Never to rise again: thy mother's poison'd:

I can no more: the king, the king's to blame.

HAMLET: The point!—envenom'd too!

Then, venom, to thy work.

[Stabs KING CLAUDIUS]

ALL: Treason! treason!

KING CLAUDIUS: O, yet defend me, friends; I am but hurt.

HAMLET: Here, thou incestuous, murderous, damned Dane,

Drink off this potion. Is thy union here?

Follow my mother.

[KING CLAUDIUS dies]

LAERTES: He is justly served;

It is a poison temper'd by himself.

Exchange forgiveness with me, noble Hamlet:

Mine and my father's death come not upon thee,

Nor thine on me.

[Dies]

HAMLET: Heaven make thee free of it! I follow thee.

I am dead, Horatio. Wretched queen, adieu!

You that look pale and tremble at this chance,

That are but mutes or audience to this act,

Had I but time—as this fell sergeant, death,

Is strict in his arrest—O, I could tell you—

But let it be. Horatio, I am dead;

Thou livest; report me and my cause aright

To the unsatisfied.

HORATIO: Never believe it:

I am more an antique Roman than a Dane:

Here's yet some liquor left.

HAMLET: As thou'rt a man,

Give me the cup: let go; by heaven, I'll have't.

O good Horatio, what a wounded name,

Things standing thus unknown, shall live behind me!

If thou didst ever hold me in thy heart

Absent thee from felicity awhile,

And in this harsh world draw thy breath in pain,

To tell my story.

March afar off, and shot within

What warlike noise is this?

OSRIC: Young Fortinbras, with conquest come from Poland,

To the ambassadors of England gives

This warlike volley.

HAMLET: O, I die, Horatio;

The potent poison quite o'er-crows my spirit:

I cannot live to hear the news from England;

But I do prophesy the election lights

On Fortinbras: he has my dying voice;

So tell him, with the occurrents, more and less,

Which have solicited. The rest is silence.

[Dies]

HORATIO: Now cracks a noble heart. Good night sweet prince:

And flights of angels sing thee to thy rest!

Why does the drum come hither?

[March within

Enter FORTINBRAS, the English Ambassadors, and others]

FORTINBRAS: Where is this sight?

HORATIO: What is it ye would see?

If aught of woe or wonder, cease your search.

FORTINBRAS: This quarry cries on havoc. O proud death,

What feast is toward in thine eternal cell,

That thou so many princes at a shot

So bloodily hast struck?

FIRST AMBASSADOR: The sight is dismal;

And our affairs from England come too late:

The ears are senseless that should give us hearing,

To tell him his commandment is fulfill'd,

That Rosencrantz and Guildenstern are dead:

Where should we have our thanks?

HORATIO: Not from his mouth,

Had it the ability of life to thank you:

He never gave commandment for their death.

But since, so jump upon this bloody question,

You from the Polack wars, and you from England,

Are here arrived give order that these bodies

High on a stage be placed to the view;

And let me speak to the yet unknowing world

How these things came about: so shall you hear

Of carnal, bloody, and unnatural acts,

Of accidental judgments, casual slaughters,

Of deaths put on by cunning and forced cause,

And, in this upshot, purposes mistook

Fall'n on the inventors' reads: all this can I

Truly deliver.

FORTINBRAS: Let us haste to hear it,

And call the noblest to the audience.

For me, with sorrow I embrace my fortune:

I have some rights of memory[7] in this kingdom,

Which now to claim my vantage doth invite me.

HORATIO: Of that I shall have also cause to speak,

And from his mouth whose voice will draw on more;

But let this same be presently perform'd,

Even while men's minds are wild; lest more mischance

On plots and errors, happen.

FORTINBRAS: Let four captains

Bear Hamlet, like a soldier, to the stage;

For he was likely, had he been put on,

To have proved most royally: and, for his passage,

The soldiers' music and the rites of war

Speak loudly for him.

Take up the bodies: such a sight as this

Becomes the field, but here shows much amiss.

Go, bid the soldiers shoot.

[A dead march.

***Exeunt, bearing off the dead bodies; after which a peal of ordnance is
shot off]***

---

[7] A fairly Deus Ex Machina end to the political subplot of our story. Due to some ancient rights of succession that Fortinbras just now happens to remember, he becomes the new ruler in Denmark following the death of King Claudius, and subsequently, Hamlet.

ACT V ASSESSMENT

After much delay, the final scenes of Act V deliver the exciting conclusion to all of the stories that have been laid before us. Hamlet finally gets his revenge, although it also means his own death. It was common in Shakespearean tragedies to have all characters die at the end, so such an ending is expected. And yet, it still feels full of high stakes and climatic action!

Now is the time to think about resolution. Hamlet achieved his revenge, but lost everything in the process. Was it worth it? Did he have any other alternatives? For this young man who craved death and madness, he appeared to have found them both.

CONCLUSION

Congratulations! You've finally read *Hamlet!* (That wasn't too bad, was it?) Now you know what you've been missing out on all along, and now you know why this play holds such an important place in the English literary canon. It's exciting. It's dramatic. It's heartfelt and there's also a touch of something poignant in it as well.

Now that you are well-versed in the text of the play, we encourage you to find a dramatic performance to watch. Chances are, there is a performance of *Hamlet* happening now or in the works for somewhere close to you, even if it's just your local high school putting on a show.

What you will find is that each interpretation of the story changes from performance to performance, sometimes in large ways and sometimes in smaller ones. It can be fun to develop a favorite moment or scene and then compare how actors and stage productions choose how to approach it. Before long, you could become a *Hamlet* expert yourself!

Keep reading for some engaging topics of discussion to introduce in your reading groups. Or if you are a student, feel free to incorporate some or all of these topics into an assignment.

DISCUSSION QUESTIONS

Discussion questions can also be used as paper topics for student readers.

1. Discuss the development of the idea of "things" throughout the play. When the ghost is first glimpsed by our sentry men, they refer to it as merely a "thing" ("… has this thing appear'd again to-night?") (Act I, Scene I) — an amorphous and vague term used to describe any old ambiguous object. Later in the play, Hamlet condemns the idea of King Claudius by declaring "The king is a thing" (Act IV, Scene 2). There are numerous instances throughout the play of this term "thing" being used to describe both the high and the low, both the ethereal and Heaven like (ie, "…my soul…a thing immortal") (Act I, Scene 4) as well as the base and degraded. What are some ways in which this term is contradictory? In what ways is it universally appropriate?

2. Compare and contrast Hamlet's thoughts and actions toward revenge with those of Laertes. Notice how Hamlet requires divine intervention, a few days of madness, time away in England, and then finally a sword in his hands before he is able to kill his father's murderer. Meanwhile, Laertes learns of his father's death, quickly rallies followers to his cause, and marches on the kingdom What can we assess from the comparison of these two figures, these two sons of murdered fathers? What do their similarities and/or differences reveal about the nature of pain and grief? About thought and action?

3. As we all know, Hamlet asks "To be or not to be?" (Act III, Scene 1). However, by the end, he has answered his own question in the form of "Let be." (Act V, Scene 2). Discuss the development of his answer as seen through the action of the play. How does he make the transition from uncertain to certain? What does this personal journey of his reveal about the larger nature of the themes he struggles with?

REFERENCES AND RESOURCES FOR FURTHER READING

Eliot, T.S. *Hamlet and His Problems*. Annotated Editions, 2019. eBook.

Shakespeare, William. Hudson, Henry Norman. *The Complete Works of William Shakespeare*. Boston: Ginn & Company. 1899. Print.

Shakespeare, William, Ann Thompson, and Neil Taylor. *Hamlet*. London: Arden Shakespeare, 2006. Print.

Shakespeare, William, and Robert S. Miola. *Hamlet: Text of the Play, the Actors' Gallery, Contexts, Criticism, Afterlives, Resources*. New York: W.W. Norton & Co, 2011. Print.

If you found this text helpful, please leave a review!